STANTON'S

SECRET
SECRET
SECRET

PATRICK GLOUTNEY

To my loving Grandmother — Dorothy Gloutney

You're always the hero of your own story, even if you are the villain — Anonymous

WCN *Stanton*

As he stepped through the watertight door, Vincent Travis rubbed his eyes in exhaustion. It was hour fourteen of what was supposed to be a ten-hour shift, but the bilge inspection had taken longer than anticipated. He stretched his neck and put away his tools. He and the rest of the skeleton crew had been busy prepping for the *Stantons'* upcoming dry dock and ultimate decommissioning. Once the pride and joy of the Western Council Navy, the *Stanton,* an advanced weapons testbed for more military projects than Vincent cared to remember, was showing its age. Despite his long service on the ship, he had been glad when its retirement had been announced. The ship was long overdue for repairs, leaving Vincent and the rest of the crew stretched thin on its last few short deployments.

Throughout its testing, the *Stanton* retained each successful weapon. Specializing in armed escort, it had seen its fair share of combat, becoming one of the deadliest and most efficient warships in the military.

"Ah, there you are!" A voice Vincent hadn't heard in years called out as he walked onto the upper decks.

"Reed?" Vince asked as the man came into view. "Weren't you reassigned?"

Spencer Reed, the former Project Manager for the *Stanton,* shook his head, "Promoted."

Vincent chuckled, "Well, what can I do for you then?"

"How's the ship holding up?"

Vincent arched an eyebrow, "It's on its last legs. It's about time they retired it."

"The hull still good?" Reed pushed.

"The whole ship is rusty and weakening."

Spencer nodded and pointed to two bluefins extending from the super-structure, "Those still work?"

Vincent winced, "As far as I know. Why do you want to know?"

"Have they been used since the incident?" Reed asked, ignoring Vincent's question.

"No. Reed what do you really want?" Vincent pushed, refusing to relive the memories of that day.

Reed was quiet for a moment. "They are giving her a new crew."

Vincent shook his head, "No. Absolutely not, the ship is too old. Besides, no one knows how to take care of it."

"You do," Reed remarked.

Vincent held up his hands, "Oh hell no. Not again. I am not taking this rust bucket on some half-thought-out mission. No, thank you, sir."

Reed chuckled, "You know it's not an option. We wouldn't be sending the ship if it weren't important. We need your help on this one. You need to keep the *Stanton* sailing."

"Send *Express* or some more modern ship."

Reed was silent for a moment. "They aren't properly equipped."

"The hell does that mean? We have the same equipment unless you..." Vincent trailed off, "Have you gone mad?"

"The new Captain will be briefed on how to work with you. You will set sail in two weeks to escort an important group of Western diplomats for the signing of a peace treaty with the Eastern Coalition. This is a big risk, but if it pays off, 50 years of conflict over ideologies will be over."

"You're dreaming, Reed. We've been at war for decades because of their resistance to change and radical views, and now they just give in suddenly and want it to stop?"

"It's far more complicated than that, but trust me, this will work. I've overseen it personally." Reed pushed.

Vincent shook his head. "Why are you doing this? It's a death sentence to anyone onboard."

Reed sighed, "Orders Vince. I wish I had a better excuse."

Patrick Gloutney

Phantom Two

Tyler "Strafer" Hale pulled his stealth fighter around in a circle, cursing his colleague in Phantom Three. They had been flying in formation, and the other pilot had mismanaged his controls, nearly knocking Tyler and their lead out of the sky.

"Phantoms regroup," the lead ordered, irritation clear in his voice. Strafer, his wingman, Nevin "Gypsy" Peterson, and their lead, Aaron "Telos" Perez, were flying advanced stealth fighters known as the PT45 Phantom attack interceptors. They were almost undetectable, but their maneuverability needed work. Their controls were so complex that it had taken countless hours of training to get any good at flying them. Gypsy was still struggling with handling the aircraft.

The joys of being a test pilot, Strafer thought to himself as he maneuvered back into formation. Today, they were pitting their aircraft against a recently revealed addition to the Western Council Aerial Test Base. Strafer didn't know much about their opponent except that it was bigger and less maneuverable than they were. It was supposed to be a strategic stealth infiltration bomber/fighter, though the information about the project was sparse.

"You boys ready for some fun?" Telos asked.

"Hell Yah," Gypsy answered.

"Always," Strafer called. He let a smile cross his face. It would be the first time they had had a challenge in the new aircraft. So far, no actual simulated engagements had been flown.

"Western Air Command *Feather's Edge* is ready to fight," a female pilot radioed.

"Roger *Feather's Edge*, Phantom Flight, are you prepared to engage?" the controller asked.

"Affirmative," Telos answered.

"Games hot then," the controller ordered. The Phantoms quickly set to work searching for the other aircraft. Tyler smiled as they worked, but as minutes ticked by with no sign of the other aircraft, his smile began to fade.

"You see him yet?" Tyler asked his radio operator or Weapons System Officer, or W.S.O., Lee "Jayhawk" Contreras.

"Nah, not yet," Jayhawk answered.

Tyler scanned the horizon before returning his attention to the other fighters in the formation. That's when movement caught his eye. He looked back and his jaw dropped.

"They're coming right for us!" Gypsy radioed, and before anyone could react, *Feather's Edge* flew over the formation, clearing their tails by a mere few meters.

"Holy shit, that was close," Jayhawk yelled.

"Break!" Telos called, and the Phantoms scattered as *Feather's Edge* circled back. Tyler yanked his aircraft around, carefully handling the controls so as not to stall the temperamental aircraft. Even so, his maneuver was tight, and as he came out of the turn, he was greeted with a surprising sight. *Feather's Edge* was diving after Phantom Three.

"Son of a bitch, she's fast," Jayhawk remarked.

"No kidding," Tyler rolled over into a dive as he spotted Telos heading after *Feather's Edge*.

I thought we were intercepting it, but Tyler fell back into formation.

"Phantom Three is dead," Gypsy radioed as he broke left leaving *Feather's Edge* to contend with his teammates. Tyler and Telos followed the new aircraft down to the hard deck altitudes for the exercise, where it tried to speed away from them.

Tyler smirked as they quickly caught up as it didn't have the speed of a Phantom. It was an odd-looking aircraft, looking more like an old V-22 Osprey than a stealth bomber. It had two large turboprop engines mounted on each wing. The engines faced forward with massive propellers barely clearing the fuselage.

"I can't lock it," Jayhawk remarked.

"What?" Something with that big a propeller disk on each engine should have bounced radar waves like a pinball machine. It was then that *Feather's Edge* pulled into a 90-degree left bank. It swung around so tightly that it was able to get behind the Phantoms.

Before they could react, Telos broke off, calling, "Phantom one's dead. She's all yours, Strafer."

Great, Tyler thought as he punched his throttles forward and pulled a tight climbing turn away from the ground. Much to his surprise, *Feather's Edge* managed to follow him, staying behind him the whole time.

"They're good," Tyler muttered as he made many attempts to shake them. While he prevented them from getting a missile lock, he wasn't able to escape.

"You're better," Jayhawk reminded him.

"Damn right I am," Tyler answered as he pulled into a near-vertical climb. Jayhawk let out a war cry as they pulled nearly 5 Gs. There was no way that aircraft could follow that. He rolled out of the climb once he ran out of energy.

"Find them quickly, Jayhawk, I—" Tyler we interrupted by the missile lock tone sounding. He looked behind him and sure enough, *Feather's Edge* was right on their tail.

"No freaking way," Jayhawk breathed.

"How did they pull that?"

"Got you Phantom Two," a gentle voice announced as *Feather's Edge* flashed its landing lights. Tyler froze. He knew that voice.

WCN *Stanton*

"Does it always do that?" the Assistant Chief Engineer, Harris, asked.

Vincent looked up from his panel. "Do what?"

"The squeaking and groaning."

Vincent nodded, going back to study the engine pressures, "Yep. As long as Righty is making noise, we are good."

"And if it stops?" Harris asked.

"Run," Vincent answered curtly.

Harris nodded, glancing nervously at the starboard engine, "You going to stare at that panel the whole trip?"

"I don't like the temperatures on the port engine," Vincent answered simply. The engines were one of the many improvements tested by the *Stanton*. At the time, they were fast, efficient, and quiet. A loud moan echoed through the engine compartment, speaking to the state of the engines now. Vincent was pretty sure he had replaced every part on either engine at least a couple of times.

"Are the rumours true?" Harris asked.

Vincent sighed; he knew the rumours about the ship's past would get out, but he hadn't expected it to spread so quickly. It must have been more notorious than he had thought.

"Chief Engineer Travis to forward decks," the intercom sounded, saving Vincent from Harris's questions.

"Watch them while I'm gone," Vincent ordered before quickly making his way to the forward decks.

He was met by Captain Delmar standing in front of the forward deck gun. About a dozen or so sailors were gathered around the gun, working on it. Over the bow, the rest of the battle group could be seen. The escort group was made up of three vessels. The flagship and group command vessel, named the *Juliane,* led the pack crashing through the surf. It was a truly menacing battleship, big and heavy with five large deck guns and multiple smaller anti-aircraft cannons covering the ship, making it look like a floating sea urchin. While the *Juliane* was a battering ram, it lacked maneuverability compared to the *Lancer.* Carrying a lighter armament, advanced engines, and a thin profile, the *Lancer* could outrun and outmaneuver almost anything on water. The *Stanton* and the *Lancer* were flanking the vessel they were escorting, the *Oscoda,* an unassuming transport vessel that was heavily armoured but not well-armed. It was a tank built to batten down its hatches and ride out an attack while the escorts dealt with any threats.

"Captain, what are they doing?" Vincent asked.

"Travis," Captain Delmar answered. Vincent wasn't sure what to make of the man yet. He seemed capable, but obviously felt at a disadvantage commanding the *Stanton* when he spoke with Vincent. It left for an awkward conversation. "The gun is jammed."

Travis nodded, "Yes. It is."

"Can we fix it?" Delmar asked.

Travis raised an eyebrow, "It hasn't moved in years."

"That doesn't answer my question."

"Not if they break it any further," Travis said, motioning to the crew working on it. As if to prove his point, the gun let out a painful groan.

"Stop!" he shouted to the crews.

"They are following orders, Mr. Travis," Delmar interjected.

"A stuck gun is better than an inoperative gun, is it not?" As if to prove his point, the gun shrieked, and one of the three barrels broke loose. The only problem was that Vincent knew the gears responsible for holding the barrel up were shot. It came crashing down on the side of the ship, crushing part of the forward gunwales. Vince and Delmar rushed to the edge of the ship as the barrel broke free from its base and tipped forward overboard. The barrel struck the side of the ship on the way down, breaching the hull above the waterline.

"Great, just great," Vincent grumbled.

"Is that normal, Mr. Travis?" Delmar asked.

"Captain, if I may make a request?"

"Go ahead,"

"Before ordering troubleshooting like that, please consult me," Vincent insisted.

"I do not see how—"

"I jammed the gun years ago on purpose," Vincent interrupted. The captain raised an eyebrow, "The system responsible for moving the guns was worn out, and I was worried that it would happen. The captain at the time and I both agreed that locking them in place was the best course of action."

"And the hull breach?" the captain inquired.

"There are more patches than hull at this point."

Patrick Gloutney

Western Council Aerial Test Base

"How'd it go, Strafer?" one of the system technicians, Marcel, asked.

"Not great," He muttered.

"By not great you mean we got our asses handed to us," Jayhawk piped up as he climbed down the ladder.

"Seriously? How long was the engagement?"

"Maybe two minutes," Tyler answered as he watched *Feather's Edge* come in for a landing. It pulled into a hover over the runway, its engines tilting upwards before settling gently on the runway.

"It's a V-TOL?" Jayhawk asked, "What kind of bomber is that thing?"

Marcel shrugged, "Your guess is as good as mine. No one will read me in. You know anything Tyler?"

Tyler didn't answer. The fact that *Feather's Edge* was capable of Vertical Take-Off and Landings was inconsequential to him. What bothered him the most was that he knew the voice he had heard over the radio.

"Well, that, gentlemen, is how you get killed on a combat mission," Lewis "Punt" Huber, Telos's W.S.O., remarked as he and the other Phantom crew walked up.

Jeffery "Rider" Frye, Gypsy's W.S.O. scoffed, "We never stood a chance against that thing." The Phantom crews watched as *Feather's Edge* finished its shutdown. As the crew walked out, Tyler shook his head when he saw the woman he knew.

"Hey Strafer, it's that the girl you've been seeing?" Jayhawk remarked. Tyler nodded.

"You mean Claire?" Punt asked. Tyler nodded again, "You're kidding. We just got destroyed by that airhead?"

"She's not an airhead," Tyler quickly defended.

"Did you know she was a pilot?" Rider asked.

"He was too busy with other things. Weren't you?" Jayhawk said with a smirk.

Tyler shook his head. "She told me she was a systems analyst. Excuse me." Tyler walked briskly up to Claire O'Reilly.

"I'm telling you the rotor response was off. She didn't pull into that climb as easily as she should have," Claire was saying as Tyler approached.

"Feather," another woman said, "It isn't even designed to pull a maneuver like that."

Claire rolled her eyes. "She's not designed for half the maneuver I put her through."

"You're impossible...Who's he?"

Claire turned and smiled, "Strafer! Did you enjoy the game?"

"You could say that. I didn't realize you were a pilot," Tyler remarked.

"Well, you know how it is. Need to know," Claire remarked, scratching the back of her neck.

"Would have thought I'd have needed to know that," Tyler remarked bitterly. He had asked what her position was, and she had blatantly lied to his face. The props on *Feather's Edge* seemed to shift suddenly as Claire deflated; she led him away to the other side of the aircraft.

"Are you angry?" she asked.

Tyler sighed, "I'm not happy you lied."

"Tyler, I had to. Those were my orders," Claire tried to explain.

He doubted that. "You never had to tell me what you were flying."

Claire bit her lip and, for some reason, it seemed like *Feather's Edge* sank into its suspension behind her, "I guess you're right. Sorry?"

Tyler shook his head, "It's a surprise, that's all. You know I don't like surprises."

Claire nodded, "Are we still on for this Friday? I can try and make it up to you?"

Tyler let a bitter smile on his face, "Sounds good."

Patrick Gloutney

WCN *Stanton*

Delmar stared out the windows of the bridge into the night. A modern ship would have had night vision onboard, but not the *Stanton*. He drummed his fingers on the station in front of him. The *Stanton* troubled him. Any other ship of that age and state of disrepair would have been retired long ago, but for some reason, the military kept extending the service life of this vessel. It made him think he was missing something, and he hated not knowing everything about his ship.

"What do you think of this?" his Executive Officer, LeCroix, asked, handing him the maintenance report from Chief Engineer Travis. The maintenance crew had managed to repair the hull breach and make the forward gun serviceable, though it was still stuck in one position. There were several other small items they had been addressing, such as the lighting in the galley. It was unsettling how easily things seemed to break on this warship.

"I'm not a fan, but we will have to make do," Delmar stated, looking to the lights of the other ships in the escort group.

"I don't know if I want to see this ship in combat," LeCroix stated with a sigh.

"She has quite the record," Delmar offered.

"Had," the X. corrected. Delmar nodded. The ship didn't seem to live up to its reputation. The mere sight of it used to send Eastern Coalition ships running. Now it seemed almost laughable. A chime brought the attention of the two men to the weapons panel.

"New surface contact bearing zero-one-zero at..." the operator trailed off.

"Distance?" Delmar asked.

"Unavailable."

"Great," Le Croix remarked, "Are we expecting company?"

"No," Delmar stated, "No one is even supposed to know where we are."

"Two more contacts...no, make that three more airborne contacts, same bearing, closing fast," the operator called.

"Damn it," Delmar cursed, "It's a goddamn ambush. Battle Stations!" The battle station chime sounded through the bridge. "Radio the *Juliane* for orders. Have all guns at the ready."

A formation of high-speed aircraft sped overhead before disappearing back into the night. Their afterburners, like tail lights in the sky, were the only indications they were there.

"We're cleared to fire," LeCroix reported. Before Delmar could make an order, an explosion erupted near the center of the escort group. The sea around them lit on fire, illuminating each ship in an eerie light.

"What kind of attack was that?" LeCroix asked.

Delmar shook his head, "They were just marking the targets for the bomber. Full speed ahead!"

Searchlights lit the night sky from the other ships as the convoy steamed ahead, trying to get away from the fires. Delmar noticed a light up ahead. He squinted through the windows, trying to make it out, only to see it glow bright and flash before disappearing. Puzzled, he looked at the rest of the convoy only to see all the lights go out before the *Stanton* suddenly started pulling ahead. He quickly realized that the other ships had all stopped.

What the hell are they doing? he asked himself. He expected any second to see the *Juliane* raise their guns, but the ships just sat there, along with all the others, motionless, not a single light on.

"Damn it. Circle back for a defensive position," Delmar ordered. The *Stanton* began pulling around just as the bombers arrived. The first bomb hit its mark. The explosion ripped a massive hole in the *Juliane's* decks.

More bombs fell, striking the bow of the *Lancer* and just missing the *Stanton*. The proximity of the detonations threw the *Stanton* off to the side. The *Stantons'* guns fired into the night sky but seemed to not affect the bombers as they disappeared for another pass.

"Damage report," Delmar commanded. "And would someone please get hold of the *Juliane!*"

"Sir," LeCroix called, pointing to the *Juliane*. Delmar grimaced at what he saw. Their flagship sat burning with a heavy list to one side. It looked as though the entire upper deck was on fire, and the superstructure was missing. The ship was lost. Delmar looked to the *Lancer*, fire raged on its bow, but it wasn't nearly as damaged, yet it sat still and dark.

"The hell is going on?" Delmar demanded. Then the *Stanton* slowed drastically.

"Port engine just stopped," LeCroix called.

"Airborne contacts are circling for another run," the radar operator called.

Delmar reached for the intercom, "I need that engine, Mr. Travis."

There was a delay, but finally, a response came: "A fuel line burst. We had to shut off its supply."

"Any fire."

"It's contained for now," Travis responded.

Delmar shook his head. He looked back at the rest of the battle group. "Where are those bombers heading?"

"Right for us," the radar operator answered. Delmar looked at the ship they were escorting. It sat undamaged in the water, motionless.

They are gunning for us, not the diplomats. He thought, "Mr. Travis, how quickly can you shut down all electrical power to the ship's lights?"

"Five minutes?" Travis responded.

"Kill them on my call," Delmar ordered. "The rest of you, I want all radar, radio, everything off after the bombers' next pass." The bridge crew acknowledged the command.

LeCroix raised an eyebrow, "For what purpose, Sir?"

"We are to play dead, LeCroix. I doubt those bombers have much reserve this far out. Convince them they have disabled us, and hopefully they leave."

"And if they don't?" LeCroix asked.

"Every plan has risks," Delmar answered simply.

"Contacts ten seconds out!" the radar operator shouted.

"I hope you are right," LeCroix muttered. The bombers bolted overhead, raining bombs on them.

"Full right rudder! Full reverse on the right engine!" Delmar commanded. The *Stanton* slowed drastically before veering off track and reversing through the waves. The bombs missed, rocking the ship with the shock waves of the explosions through the water.

"Now, Mr. Travis!" Delmar called over the intercom. With that, every light went out. "All Stop. Engine's off, Mr. Travis."

"Sir, I advise—"

"Engine's off, Mr. Travis." Delmar insisted.

"Yes, Sir," Travis stated, and the intercom clicked off. Silence filled the bridge as the bombers made a third pass, only this time they didn't drop any payload. They flew over the *Stanton* before banking back towards land.

Delmar let out a sigh of relief as their lights disappeared into the darkness. His reprieve was short-lived, however, as a mighty groan pierced the air. Delmar looked back in time to see the *Juliane* rolling onto her side.

Western Council Aerial Test Base

"You don't understand!" Claire "Feather" Valdes's angered voice seeped through the door to the Project Coordinator's office. Sam "Greaser" Marshall flinched. Sam was the Flight Engineer on board *Feather's Edge*. She had known Feather for years, even before the project had messed with her head. She'd helped her get over some personal hardship and got her into the military with her. But she had never heard her raise her voice like this.

"You don't even care!"

Sam looked to *Feather Edge's* W.S.O., Gabby "Flint" Keller, and raised an eyebrow.

"Hell, if I know," Flint answered.

"You don't think she's still arguing with him about the turbine response time, do you?" Sam asked.

"Hope not," Flint grunted, "They already managed to reduce it by 10%."

At that moment, the door to the coordinator's office flew open, and a seething Feather marched out. She spoke to no one as she stormed outside.

"Wow, I haven't ever seen her that steamed," Flint remarked.

Sam nodded and looked at the coordinator, "What did you do?"

The Coordinator, General Boudreaux, shook his head, "She wants to read one of the Phantoms in on her condition."

"Why?" Sam asked.

"Personal Reasons," Boudreaux said, making air quotes with his hands.

"Hope you said no," Flint stated.

"Flint!" Sam chastised.

"Hey, I'm just saying. The fewer people who know about her, the better."

Boudreaux nodded, "I agree."

"You know she's more than just a project," Sam pointed out. Before anyone else could speak, Boudreaux's phone rang.

He looked at Sam after he hung up, "*Feather's Edge* is locked up. Greaser, can you go deal with Feather?"

"We didn't name that plane after her for nothing," Sam stated as she went to find Feather, "She's got this project by the throat and you know it."

It didn't take long. She was just outside the hangar, staring across the tarmac towards *Feather's Edge.* "Feather?" Sam called as she walked up behind the pilot. She could hear the woman sniffle as she tried to dry her eyes.

"I take it you heard me," Feather remarked, her voice heavy.

Sam placed a hand on her shoulder, "Yeah, we all did. What's wrong?"

"Nothing that matters," Feather remarked.

"I'd say it matters to you," Sam argued.

"So?"

"Then it matters to me," Sam reassured, "Now why don't you tell me what all the shouting was about?"

"I asked if I could read Strafer in on my condition," Feather answered.

Sam nodded, "I take it the answer was no." Feather nodded, "Why does Strafer need to know?"

"Because..." Feather trailed off, "Oh, right, I haven't told you."

Sam tilted her head, "Told me what?"

"I've been seeing someone..." Feather mumbled.

Sam's eyes went wide, "Damn girl! That's great! Strafer?" Feather nodded. "How long?"

"A while. We met online at first..." Feather mumbled.

Sam patted Feather on the head, "Must be serious if you want to tell him."

Feather sighed, "He wasn't happy with me after we beat the Phantoms."

"Why?"

"I didn't tell him I was a pilot," Feather answered and then choked up, "I lied right to his face when he asked."

"Oh, Feather," Sam pulled her friend into a hug, "He'll get over it."

Feather shook her head, "He wanted two things from me: honesty and trust. I broke both in one sentence." Feather then began beating the back of her head, "All because of this stupid chip."

Sam gently grabbed Feather's hands, "Shhh. You think reading him in will change that?"

"I don't know, but it would at least help him understand," Feather responded. "He said he was fine with it, but he felt so distant on Friday. It felt like he was slipping away. I can't lose him, Sam."

Sam chewed on her cheek for a moment, She didn't like where this was going. Feather's condition left her...vulnerable. "If he's worth your time, he'll stick around."

Feather stiffened, "You don't understand, Sam. I'm the one who's not worth his time." Sam was going to protest, but Feather continued, "I ran away from home, from my problems. I joined up to try and escape. I volunteered for this project, thinking it would make everything better, instead...it's only made it worse. I am even more of a freak than I was before."

Feather wiped her eyes, "And him...he's kind, caring, he listens to me when I rant. He doesn't mind when I space out; he's patient and has never asked for anything in return. He has called off plans with the other Phantoms just to comfort me. Hell, he walked out of a briefing for me once," Feather's voice was becoming more strained, "And all I have ever done for him is..."

Feather broke down again, tears flowing down her cheeks as Sam held her tight.

"Shh," Sam tried to comfort. "It's going to be alright. I'll make sure of it."

WCN *Stanton*

"What do you mean you can't?" LeCroix asked, leaning over the table in the briefing room.

Vincent glanced at Captain Delmar, but the man remained quiet. "To avoid carrying extra batteries, the *Stanton* was designed to use the two auxiliary diesel generators to supply power to the starter motors on each engine. Normally, one auxiliary generator would start the engines, and the other would supply power to the basic system required to get the ship underway. Right now, though, the system responsible for diverting power to the starboard engine's starter is shot. So, I can't start it."

"How did you start it back at the port?" Delmar asked, far calmer than his XO.

"Foreseeing this problem, they designed the electrical system to allow us to start either engine by diverting power from the opposite engine's main generator. It's how we've been starting the starboard engine for at least the last six months."

"So start the Port engine," LeCroix suggested.

Vincent shook his head, "Its fuel system was heavily damaged in the fight. It's out of service until we can make repairs."

"Unbelievable," LeCroix muttered.

"Why wasn't this addressed before our departure?" Delmar asked.

Vincent sighed and shook his head, "The failure of the starting system occurred during the last deployment. Given that the *Stanton* was scheduled for decommissioning, it wasn't deemed worth repairing. When it was put back into service, I didn't have time or the parts I needed since they aren't made any-more."

"Then why sail at all?" Delmar asked.

Vincent cocked his head to the side, "We were ordered, by you. Weren't you briefed on the condition of the ship?"

Delmar shook his head, "Not to this extent."

Thanks, Reed, Vincent thought to himself, "Then you are in for a few surprises. Given the orders and the fact, we have never shut both engines down on deployment due to their long warm-up period I deemed it safe for service."

Delmar leaned forward, rubbing his temples, "Alright. I want a report of every nuance I should know about. How long until the Port engine can be repaired?"

Vincent winced, "At least two days."

"What?" LeCroix demanded.

"The repair isn't exceedingly complicated, but I need manpower and right now, my crew is stretched thin repairing the leaks and minor hull breaches we've accumulated on account of the fight," Vincent explained.

"So you're sinking?" Captain Hernandez of the *Lancer* remarked. He had been invited to join in the briefing as they tried to figure out their next course of action.

"No," Vincent stressed, "I knew we'd have hull problems; I did manage to get two additional bilge pumps installed before our departure, along with a few portable ones brought on board. Right now, they are keeping up at only 40% capacity. Once the hull repairs are done, we can focus on the engines."

Delmar nodded with a sigh, "That about covers the status of our ship. How's the *Lancer*?"

Hernandez grimaced, "Out of commission. Every electrical system we have is fried and with how reliant the ship is on automation we can't do anything."

"Does it have a manual reversion mode?" Vincent asked, looking out the porthole at the *Lancer*.

"We are working on it. Some of the weapons can be operated without computers, but the tracking systems won't work. My Chief Engineer is also looking at our engines, but it's not likely we will be able to get them running. They have more computers on them than almost any part of the ship."

Vincent shook his head. The joys of modern ships, computers made for an efficient and well-run ship, as long as they worked.

"Any idea as to what hit you?" Delmar asked.

"Likely an EMP," Vincent stated without thinking.

He saw Hernandez raise an eyebrow, "My Engineer said the same thing, except for the fact that an EMP blast would have had the same effect on the *Stanton,* and, despite your condition, your electrical systems seem fine."

Vincent nodded, "Normally, yes, but the *Stanton* was built to be impervious to Electro-Magnetic Pulse attacks. It would explain the sudden stop of both the *Lancer* and the *Juliane*. I assume the *Oscoda* likewise reported similar damage."

Delmar nodded, "Why such a specific protection?"

"One of the many weapons onboard is an EMP generator," Vincent explained.

"I saw no mention of that in the ship's file," Delmar remarked.

"Like I said, Sir," Vince answered, "Surprises."

Patrick Gloutney

Western Council Command Center

"What do we know?" Tasia Whiteford asked as she took her seat at the head of the table, flipping open the file in front of her.

"Reports show it was a multi-wave, long-range, well-coordinated attack. The initial wave was an EMP blast followed by subsequent bombing runs to disable the escorting ships. No further attack has been made and the intentions of the aggressor are unclear," the head of Military Operations, Commander Gareth Bell, explained.

"Status on the *Oscoda*?"

"The *Oscoda* was disabled but otherwise undamaged," the man responded.

"Do we know who attacked the escort group?"

"No, Ma'am," the Intelligence Officer answered, "We weren't watching the formation when—"

Tasia put up her hand, stopping the Intelligence Officer, "Weren't you watching them?"

"Er...yes ma'am."

"The single most important diplomatic mission in the last decade, and they were operating blind?" Tasia watched as the Intelligence Officer squirmed under her gaze for a moment before continuing, "Do we have eyes on them now?" The Officer shook his head, "Then you best get your people working on it."

The man nodded, "Yes, ma'am."

Tasia nodded and skimmed through her report; no one dared to interrupt her. A frown etched itself deeper on her face.

Lancer: DISABLED – REPAIR STATUS UNKNOWN
Oscoda: DISABLED – REPAIR STATUS UNKNOWN
Juliane: DESTROYED – LOST AT SEA
Stanton: DISABLED – REPAIRS UNDERWAY

"Commander Bell, why do I see the *Stanton* on this report? It was to be dismantled, was it not?"

Bell nodded, "It was a last-minute addition to the escort group. The diplomats refused to go unless protected by the *Stanton*, its reputation reassured them somewhat."

"And why wasn't the *Stanton* able to defend the escort group? It can fight in EMP warfare, can it not?"

Bell coughed, "I'm afraid due to the nature of its deployment, there was insufficient time to train the crew on its...unique armament."

Tasia leaned back in her chair, pinching the bridge of her nose, "So let me get this straight. We send our most advanced escort vessels and a heavily armoured transport vessel on a very important diplomatic mission. One that will end the war. They are attacked while running blind without our help, and the only somewhat operational one left is a rust bucket that was, and I quote, 'going to fall apart if we deployed it again', that no one knows how to sail?" The glances her Senior Commanders gave each other told Tasia all she needed to know. It was then that she noticed the man silently sitting in the corner. "You are all dismissed."

As the Commanders filed out of the room, she looked to the man in the corner, "You hear about the attack or funding, Mr. Reed?"

"The attack," General Spencer Reed, Commander of the Advanced Technology Division, responded.

Tasia glanced at her watch. "You have one minute to impress me before I send you back to the desert."

Reed nodded, "The *Stanton* can protect the diplomats till we get a rescue crew there."

"I agree. But no one knows how to use her weapons," Tasia countered.

Reed handed her a file, "Vincent Travis does. He's been on board most of his career. Built most of the weapons."

Tasia flipped open the file and scanned the information, "Ok, my interest's piqued. What are you proposing?"

"Do you recall the Phantom and Feather projects?" Reed asked.

Tasia nodded, "Vaguely. You have quite a few."

"I've put the projects against one another to see how they work together. I hope to deploy them together."

"An odd combination. A fast fighter, and a cumbersome bomber?" Tasia remarked.

"*Feather's Edge* is far from cumbersome, but that's not the point. I paired them because the technology in the *Stanton*'s EMP resistance was used in both their designs," Reed explained.

Tasia looked back up over the file, "Now that is interesting; you want me to send them on a rescue mission?"

Reed nodded, "We can easily reconfigure *Feather's Edge* to accommodate passengers. The Phantoms provide additional protection."

"That is a lot of people to fit on *Feather's Edge*." Tasia remarked, "You'll never get all the crew home."

"We don't need to. The *Stanton* can bring the *Lancer* and *Oscoda* crew home. *Feather's Edge* deals only with the diplomats. Brings them to a new ship, and they continue with their mission."

Tasia grimaced as she thought of something, "They would be untested."

Reed twirled a pen in his hand, "We have no alternative. Anything else we send would likely be disabled by an EMP, much like the *Lancer* was."

"How long till they can be deployed?"

"Two weeks," Reed answered, "We have to finish this round of tests and retrofit *Feather's Edge.*"

Tasia sighed; two weeks was a long time. It left the escort group vulnerable to more attacks, and it would mean a challenging negotiation with the Eastern Coalition to allow the delay in the diplomatic proceedings. "Very well. I'll contact Captain Delmar personally. You contact your man as well. We are to authorize the use of all and any weapons needed to protect the *Oscoda.*"

Reed chewed the inside of his cheek, "Does that include—"

"Yes, if it comes to it," Tasia interrupted, "Let's just hope they can hold out long enough."

WCN *Stanton*

"You can't be serious?" Vincent asked over the phone.

"It's the last resort, but yes," Reed answered.

Vincent sighed, leaning on a support beam, "Reed, you know what happened last time it was fired. I'd be slaughtering the crew again."

"Just make sure everyone is below decks," Reed suggested, "You have other weapons too."

"And the recoil from some of those weapons?" Vincent asked, "The ship is barely holding together as it is. I have no idea what condition the weapons mounts are in."

"You'll figure something out," Reed remarked, seemingly unconcerned, "You always have."

Vincent clenched his fists and let out a frustrated sigh. "How long till the reinforcements arrive?"

"Two weeks."

Vincent slammed his fist into the post, "We can't hold out that long Reed!"

"I have faith—"

"In a ship built over fifty years ago," Vincent interrupted, "Did you even inspect the ship aside from talking with me before this mission?" There was no answer from Reed. "Unbelievable."

"I understand your frustrations, Vincent, but the fact of the matter is, you are all we've got."

"No," Vincent answered, "We aren't capable of fighting. Not with a rusted-out husk of a ship and a crew that doesn't know a thing about how to sail it." Vincent slammed the phone onto its cradle and rested both hands on the post, arms shaking. He let out heavy breaths and shook his head. He reached up to his pocket and withdrew the photograph he kept there. He grimaced at the memories it brought forth.

Memories of the death and destruction the *Stanton* had brought upon its crew and all those around it. They had been so stupid to fire a weapon that had never been tested. They had been desperate. Desperation had led to a poor decision; a decision that still haunted not only the Western Council Navy but Vincent himself to this day.

One shot, Vincent thought grimly. *One shot and we became a ghost ship.* A cough brought Vincent out of his musings, and he straightened up. He knew where this was going, and it was going to leave the *Stanton* desperate once again.

"Is this a bad time?" Captain Delmar asked. Vincent shook his head and put the picture away. "That your girl back home?"

"Was," Vincent said, a bitter bite to his voice, "What can I do for you, Captain?"

Delmar nodded and stepped toward the engines, "I wanted to come down and see how things are going."

"Hull repairs are coming along on schedule. Engines are next," Vincent reported automatically, following the captain.

"Relax, Mr. Travis, I'm not here for a status report. I'm here to learn."

"Pardon?"

Delmar turned to face Vincent, "I feel we got off on the wrong foot. I was as much rushed into this command as the *Stanton* was rushed back into service. Rather than address the issue, I let my disadvantage become my downfall."

Vincent nodded, "I wouldn't say downfall, sir. We are alive because of your actions."

"For now," Delmar stated, "But I'm the reason we are dead in the water. I don't intend on making such a mistake again."

"All right," Vincent said, leaning against the side of the engine, "What do you want to know?"

"I've been thinking of the EMP. It needs power, correct?" Delmar asked.

"Yes, and by that, I mean the engines. It isn't linked into the auxiliary system."

"Any chance of making such a modification?"

Vincent shook his head, "It draws too much power. We'd likely burn out the generator."

Delmar nodded, "Any chance of reducing power output to compensate?" Vincent shook his head. "I thought not. We have other weapons, right?"

Vincent ran a hand through his short-cut hair, "Yes, but they all rely on the primary generators on the engines. Nothing is linked to the auxiliary system. The *Stanton* was never designed to fight without at least one engine running."

Delmar seemed content with the answer. However, he seemed to hesitate with his next question. "May I ask what happened between you and that woman?"

"Why?"

"She served on board the *Stanton,* did she not?" Delmar pressed. "I saw the misconduct warning on your file."

Vincent sighed, "She died."

Delmar seemed to ponder this for a few moments. "Vincent, I want you to be painfully honest with me. Are the rumours about the *Stanton* true?"

Vincent nodded, "Every word. The *Stanton* killed her, and almost every other crew member on board that day."

Western Council Aerial Test Base

"You are way too worked up over this," Tyler stated as they sat in the mess hall eating what the cook had decided to pass as food for the day.

"How can you not be?" Jayhawk demanded.

Tyler shrugged, "We lost. It happens."

"And the fact we lost to Claire?" Jayhawk snapped.

Tyler arched his eyebrow, "What does it matter that it was Claire?"

Jayhawk rolled his eyes, "C'mon, Strafer. She can barely carry on a conversation without getting distracted."

"Maybe she's thinking of flying," Tyler joked.

"You're unbelievable," Jayhawk remarked, "She could probably get away with anything with you."

"What is that supposed to mean?" Tyler shot.

"C'mon, whenever your hot girlfriend calls, you come running. You even walked out on Telos during a briefing."

Tyler grimaced, maybe not his proudest moment, but the scolding he had received had been worth it. Claire had needed him, and he had been right where he had been needed. That thought brought a stab of pain to his heart. He would have given her anything, and she couldn't even be honest with him.

"It's little mystery what you're running to do," Jayhawk grumbled.

Tyler rolled his eyes. "What I do with Claire is none of your business. Besides, you're just jealous."

"I am not," Jayhawk snapped, then sighed, "Ok, maybe a little." Tyler laughed at his friend's antics.

"Strafer?" A female voice called. The two men turned to see a blond woman approaching them. "I'm Greaser, I'm a...systems analyst on *Feather's Edge.*"

"A systems analyst?" Tyler asked skeptically.

"May I speak with you in private?"

"Unbelievable," Jayhawk muttered. Tyler shot him a glare before nodding. Greaser led him outside of the mess before she turned to him.

"I want to talk about Feather."

"Ah, yes, your fellow systems analyst," Tyler remarked drily.

Greaser frowned, "Look. I am here to help. If you're going to attack Feather like that, then I will leave."

Tyler sighed, but relented, "I'm listening."

"You're mad because she lied to you, right?" Greaser asked. Tyler said nothing. "You should know she would have told you if she could have."

"She never had—"

"To tell you what she flew. Trust me, it's not that simple. What I am about to tell you cannot be repeated. It is classified information about Feather and that aircraft. Am I clear?"

"Why tell me then?" Tyler asked, crossing his arms.

"Because if you are going to be with her, you need to know," Greaser stated, "Feather is different. I'm sure you've noticed she spaces out a lot?"

Tyler nodded.

"Well, it's not because she's dumb," Greaser stressed, "Our project is not *Feather's Edge.* It is Feather. She is the first human to be cybernetically linked to a machine."

Tyler cocked his head to one side, "I'm sorry?"

"The fact that Feather's call sign and *Feather Edge's* name are so similar was done for a reason. It is Feather's *Edge* in combat. She has a cybernetic implant in her brain that links her to the aircraft. It allows *Feather's Edge* to communicate data directly to her without her having to interpret it through sight. She can feel everything: airspeed, G-loading, altitude, and engine torque values. If there is a sensor, its data is fed directly to her brain through the implant's interface."

"Sounds far-fetched," Tyler remarked.

"Everything on this base is far-fetched," Greaser countered.

"Fair point."

Greaser sighed, "Look, Strafer, there's more to it than what she can do in an aircraft. One of the side effects is that she can't turn it off. She can feel everything all the time. She spaces out because she feels something on *Feather's Edge*. It's not unlike the phantom limb syndrome that amputees experience. The aircraft is essentially a detached limb to Feather. When they do maintenance on it, she is forced to endure pain when they start fixing sensors."

Memories of comforting Claire as she had a breakdown, or was in some kind of pain, flooded Strafer's mind: "Is that why she's depressed?"

Greaser nodded, "Depressed may not be the right word, but yes. One of the other side effects is that she can be indirectly programmed because of the implant. When it comes to orders, she's forced to follow them to T. We were ordered not to tell anyone what our project was and to simply say we are systems analysts. That's why when you asked her what she did—"

"She had no choice but to lie," Tyler finished, beginning to understand.

Patrick Gloutney

WCN *Stanton*

"New airborne contacts bearing zero-one-zero," the radar operator called across the bridge.

Here we go again, Delmar thought. He knew they'd be back, but he had held out hope that he had been wrong. "Time till intercept?"

"Ten minutes, Sir."

Delmar scowled. His conversation with Mr. Travis was still at the forefront of his mind. He cued the intercom, "Any chance we can get that EMP Mr. Travis?"

"Negative," Travis's short reply came.

Delmar sighed, "Battle stations." The battle station chime sounded through the bridge as Delmar walked to the windows with a pair of binoculars. Soon enough, he could spot the incoming aircraft. Two fighters and a high-speed helicopter, from the looks of it.

"What's the chance they ignore us?" LeCroix asked.

"That would mean they are going for the *Oscoda,*" Delmar remarked.

He could see LeCroix grimace, "Chopper is a bad sign."

"It was never about sinking us. Seems they want the diplomats," Delmar agreed. He watched as the fighters peeled away from the helicopter and flew towards the *Lancer.*

"We could use that EMP, Mr. Travis," Delmar pushed.

"I'm working on it," Travis answered. The two enemy fighters shot overhead the *Lancer* at low level as if to inspect it. Seemingly satisfied, they circled towards the *Stanton*.

"What are they doing?" LeCroix remarked.

"Recon, I bet. They know we are active, but we don't have any weapon radar up. They want to make sure it's not a trap before they attack." Delmar proposed. "Do we have power to the jammers?"

LeCroix looked down at his panel, "Negative."

The fighters passed by the *Stanton* almost lower than her mainmast. Delmar did not doubt that they would quickly realize the ship wasn't quite dead yet. He watched them pull around, likely to set up for a weapons pass. Delmar surveyed the bridge; they were dead in the water with no hope of fighting back. He looked at the helicopter approaching the *Oscoda*. His orders rang clear in his ears.

Protect it at all costs, was what Whiteford had said. He had never before felt so helpless commanding a warship.

"Targets now bearing three-six-zero, closing fast."

"Everyone take cover," Delmar ordered before every display blacked out. He was about to call Travis when an alarm he had never heard sounded through the ship.

"Warning. Weapons discharge is imminent. All hands below decks," a computerized voice called.

"Sir!" LeCroix called, pointing to the bow of the ship. The forward gunwales were lifting, exposing some form of contraption underneath. Two pillars extended forward from the bow before the edges extended to form a V.

"Targets acquired," the computerized voice called. Delmar watched as the edges of the extended "V" from the bow began to glow red. Then, with a loud pop, the *Stanton* lurched backward, throwing Delmar and LeCroix to the floor.

Delmar rushed to his feet just in time to see the oncoming fighters split in two and crash into the water just before the *Stanton's* bow.

The V shifted to the left towards the *Oscoda* before the computer called, "Target Acquired." The second shot threw the *Stanton* into a yawing movement, turning the ship easily 45 degrees.

Dead silence reigned on the bridge as they watched the enemy helicopter hit the water.

Holy shit, Delmar thought to himself as the weapon they had just used retracted back into the *Stanton's* hull, the forward gunwale coming back to position. He had heard of the weapons on board the *Stanton,* and despite the confirmation he had received from Travis earlier, he still couldn't believe such weapons existed. It had sliced through the oncoming aircraft like a hot knife through butter. And the recoil was enough to move an entire battleship.

"Weapons Clear," the computer called before power was restored to the bridge.

Delmar reached for the intercom. "Well done, Mr. Travis."

"What was that?" LeCroix asked, holding his head where he had banged it during a fall.

Delmar looked out to the *Oscoda* and then back to his ship, "A surprise, LeCroix. Looks like the *Stanton* has given up one of her secrets."

Patrick Gloutney

Western Council Aerial Test Base

Tyler readjusted the last plate setting when a knock came at the door. He smiled to himself, punctual as always. He took a moment to straighten his shirt before he answered. As he opened the door, he was struck speechless.

Hot damn Claire, Claire was standing at his door, wearing possibly the sexiest dress he had ever seen. She was nervously rubbing her forearm and looking down away from him. Red flags started to pop up in Tyler's mind. Claire never dressed like this, and she looked like a puppy about to be beaten.

"Hey," she said, looking up at him.

"Hey, gorgeous," he answered back, letting her in.

Claire made her way to the table. "Did you have a good day?"

"I did actually," Tyler answered, pulling out her chair.

"Really?" Claire asked, clearly relieved, "Tell me about it."

"You don't want to hear about my boring life as a pilot of an aircraft that barely flies," Tyler joked, putting down the two plates of chicken parmesan and pasta for their dinner.

"I do, Tyler. Your days are as important to me as my own," Claire answered, "Besides, it's not like mine fly any more than yours."

"Well," Tyler started, pouring them some wine, "I started the day with some paperwork, then had a crew briefing, then more paperwork. Then we had a meeting to discuss our war game with you. Sorted out a few problems with the techs with my Phantom and I opened the door for the most beautiful woman I've ever seen."

Claire looked away with a blush, "You're such a ham."

"You love it," Tyler remarked, taking his seat across from her. Claire nodded. "So, Claire, how was yours?"

"The usual. Worked on our project. Kept busy. Lots of...systems to analyze. Issues to fix," she explained. Tyler noted how strained she looked.

"It's okay Claire. Really," Tyler stated, serving her, "You don't have to talk about your work."

"No, it's not okay," Claire muttered, "You have no way to understand."

"Maybe not, I know a little more now. Greaser explained everything to me yesterday."

Claire's head shot up, "She read you in?" Tyler nodded, "So you know about me and my connection to..."

"Yep."

"Do you think differently of me?"

"Yep."

Claire visibly deflated, "Oh."

"I think you're stronger than I ever did before," Tyler said, grasping her hand.

Claire's face lit up as she smiled, "You're terrible."

"Not as terrible as the tease sitting across from me."

Claire glanced down at her outfit, "Uhm yeah. It was Flint's idea to make it up to you."

Tyler nodded in thought before smiling, "Not exactly your style."

Claire giggled a little, "No. It's not. But...if you—"

"Not when you feel forced to," Tyler interrupted, "And we both know you'd be lying if you said otherwise right now."

The two lapsed into a comfortable silence as they ate until Strafer spoke again, "Your flying impressed me the other day."

"Oh...thanks," Claire said cautiously, "You weren't bad yourself."

Tyler grimaced, his insecurities as a pilot rearing their ugly head in his mind, "I'm not nearly as good as you, or Telos for that matter."

"From what I've heard, your aircraft isn't all it's cracked up to be," Claire remarked.

Tyler grunted in approval, "They have a few kinks to work out. But hey, keeps life interesting."

Claire looked away, seemingly deep in thought. "Tyler?"

"Yes?" he asked through a mouth full of pasta.

Claire giggled, "I think I love you."

Tyler nearly choked on a noodle. Neither of them had said that yet. He looked at Claire like a deer in the headlights.

"No. I know I love you," she said again. Again, Tyler couldn't bring himself to speak. She loved him; this beautiful, fragile creature loved him. It made his heart race just thinking about it.

Claire shifted in her seat, "Tyler...I understand if you don't, but do you love me?"

"Is the Pope Jewish?" Tyler blurted out, *Smooth idiot.*

"Uhm...the Pope is Catholic?" Claire said uneasily.

"Same difference," Tyler said a little too forcefully.

Patrick Gloutney

Western Council Aerial Test Base

"So..." Flint asked Feather with a little too much glee for Sam's taste. Feather didn't answer as she inspected the landing gear on *Feather's Edge*. Sam could hear the eye roll from Flint. She smirked a little. Feather had been quiet all morning, which was driving Flint nuts.

"You're going to make her blow a fuse, Feather," Sam remarked as she closed up an access panel after verifying their fuel was clean.

"Hmm?" Feather asked.

"C'mon," Flint groaned, "How was he?"

"Who?" Feather asked absentmindedly.

"Strafer," Flint stated flatly.

"Oh. He was nice. Had a wonderful dinner all laid out. He was very understanding. Thanks for that, by the way, Greaser," Feather explained.

Flint raised an eyebrow at Sam, "You helped?"

Sam raised her hands defensively, "Not the way you're thinking."

Flint nodded before sighing, "Feather?"

"Yes."

"Where did you sleep last night?"

"In my bed?" Feather answered, sounding confused by the question.

Flint let out a spectacular groan, "God, you two are so boring!"

Sam chuckled. Flint had been obsessing over the relationship between Feather and Strafer, but not in a cute way. "Just leave her be, Flint."

"C'mon Greaser," Flint whined, "She hid him from us so far, the least she can do is spare a few details."

"I don't think anything happened last night," Sam countered, inspecting the engines.

"Oh, I wouldn't say that," Feather chimed in.

This got Sam's attention, "Really?

"I told him I love him," Feather stated simply

"Yes! Finally getting somewhere," Flint exclaimed. Sam wasn't as excited; it could explain how quiet Feather was being.

"Did he say it back?" she asked. Feather shook her head. "Oh, Claire. I'm sorry to hear that."

"It's okay," Feather said, "He'll tell me when he's ready. I can be patient."

"Still—"

"Almost ready to go?" Boudreaux interrupted. Sam sighed and glanced at Feather; she was still doing her pre-flight seemingly without care. But Sam could see the hurt hidden behind her eyes.

"Just about," Feather answered professionally. They were supposed to be going up against the Phantoms again in a joint test. The engineers wanted to see how well *Feather's Edge* could evade, while at the same time, the crew in the Phantoms wanted another chance against Feather.

"You going easy on them?" Flint teased.

"Only in their dreams," Feather answered simply.

Phantom Two

Tyler sidled his Phantom up next to Telos' aircraft. They were flying with him and Gypsy on either side of Telos. They were planning on testing their aircraft's chasing abilities against *Feather's Edge* again today. Only this time, their opponent wouldn't shoot back, only run.

"How are your flight controls feeling, Strafer?" Telos asked.

Tyler tested his controls gently, "Normal." His Phantom had a history of malfunctions with its flight computer. It hadn't come up recently, but they had discovered the control movement limits were off in the last maintenance inspection. It had been repaired and passed its last test flight, but Telos was understandably cautious.

"Don't pull anything too crazy right away until you know you have full control of travel," Telos cautioned.

"Had a full travel the other day," Strafer answered. *Maybe too cautious.*

"All units, Hell Desert Air Command, your game is hot. Have fun," the controller stated.

"Can't wait for a rematch," Jayhawk said from the back seat.

Tyler smiled, "You're just mad we lost to a girl."

"Your girl. Does it work that way on the ground, too?" Jayhawk teased. Tyler was going to respond when *Feather's Edge* flew below them.

"Phantoms left," Telos called as he started the left-hand bank. Tyler followed along on the inside of the turn as they dove after the fleeing *Feather's Edge*. They chased in formation as *Feather's Edge* tried to evade them.

"She's freaking good," Jayhawk muttered. Tyler had to agree. *Feather's Edge* wasn't staying in one place long enough for his weapons to lock on a shot. Then she pulled into a hover.

"Break," Telos called. They scattered to avoid plowing into the hovering aircraft. Tyler broke left, pulling a tight circle. He was able to see *Feather's Edge* tip its rotors and start a spiralling descent.

"Phantom Two with me, three cut her off," Telos ordered. Tyler complied quickly, falling into position off Telos's right wing. They quickly turned after *Feather's Edge,* who by now was as low as she was allowed to go in this exercise. The fleeing aircraft was pulling tight S-turns, making it hard for the Phantoms to follow. Suddenly, it shot up into a near-vertical climb. Tyler went to pull back on his stick to follow, only for his aircraft to violently roll to the right.

"Shit," Tyler grunted as he tried to right his aircraft, "We hit her wake." Tyler fought with his controls as his aircraft rolled inverted. The nose fell into a dive. Tyler kicked his rudder and managed to get his wings to near level when his controls stopped responding.

"Strafer, you alright?" Telos asked.

"What's going on Strafer?" Jayhawk asked worriedly from the back. Tyler desperately tried to right his aircraft but it wasn't responding; they were stuck in a rapid descending turn. Even his throttles weren't responding.

"Jayhawk, give me a full system rest."

"On it boss," Jayhawk answered. The instrument panel went dark for a split second before lighting back up.

"Knock it off," Telos's call ended the exercise for the others as Tyler's controls started responding again. Tyler levelled the wings and pulled out of the dive, but it was too late.

"Tower!" Jayhawk called a second before they hit one of the tower's guy wires. The Phantom yawed drastically to the right from the impact. Tyler managed to stop it from rolling over, but just barely.

"Shit. We're losing hydraulic fluid," Jayhawk reported.

"Damn it," Tyler muttered as he started climbing. He queued his microphone, "Mayday, Mayday, Mayday Phantom Two has a flight control failure, port wing contact and is leaking hydraulics."

"Check that Phantom Two turn heading 200 for runway 28 when able."

"Telos, can you check my wing?" Tyler asked. He could already feel his controls becoming sloppy from the leaking hydraulic fluid.

"On my way," Telos called. Soon, Telos was on his left wing, an odd sight to say the least. Gypsy flew a safe distance off his left.

"You want the good or bad news?" Telos asked.

"Both,"

"Your ailerons are not jammed."

"That's good," Tyler noted.

"That bird will never land, though. Your wings are too damaged to support you at low speeds."

"Fuck," Tyler swore, "Jayhawk, how much longer till we are out of hydraulics?"

"Maybe a minute at this rate." Tyler scanned up ahead. There was plenty of flat space, but if they couldn't slow down, they couldn't extend their landing gear. If they couldn't do that, they would have to belly it at high speeds. There was no way they would survive that.

"We're going to have to—" Before Tyler could finish his sentence, his aircraft rolled to the left away from Telos. Tyler tried to right it, but it was no use. He glanced at his altimeter. They were too low to reset the system.

"Get out Jayhawk!" he shouted. "Punch out!" He reached for his ejection handles. He heard the canopy blow off and Jayhawk's seat fire. He waited until his aircraft had rolled upright again and pulled his handles.

Patrick Gloutney

Feather's Edge

Sam smiled as Feather rotated the engines on their aircraft upwards, pulling it into a near-vertical climb. *Good luck following that one, boys,* she thought to herself. They hadn't been at the war game very long, but it was clear that the Phantoms weren't going to land any hits on them. Feather kept their climb going before levelling off and rolling into a tight turn in the opposite direction.

"You got position reports for me, Flint?" Feather asked as Sam quickly scanned their instruments to make sure everything was in order.

"Phantom One's pulling left but not chasing, and looks to be regrouping with Phantom Three. Phantom Two is..." Flint trailed off.

Sam glanced at Feather, "Where's Phantom Two?"

"He's diving."

"What?" Feather asked.

"Knock it off" came through on the radio, and Sam could see Feather tense.

"Flint, what is Strafer doing?"

"I don't know. He'd better pull up soon, though."

Sam noticed Feather nervously tapping the throttles. "Relax, Feather, he knows what he's doing."

The next radio call, however, did not help: "Mayday, Mayday, Mayday Phantom Two has a flight control failure, port wing contact and is leaking hydraulics."

"Or not," Flint remarked, "Damn looks like he hit a tower at the bombing range."

"No, that can't be right," Feather muttered, "How is he still flying?"

"Must have hit the guy wires," Flint remarked.

Sam glanced at her instruments, she noticed that the engine's internal turbine temperature, or ITT, was fluctuating more than normal, "Easy Feather. He'll be fine."

Feather wasn't listening as she turned the Phantom frequency into one of the radios, "That bird will never land, though. Your wings are too damaged to support you at low speeds."

Feather flinched, and the number two engine flamed out.

"Number two flame out," Sam called, but there was no response from Feather.

"Gypsy break, he's rolling!" Telos's voice called over the radio as the yaw from the lost engine began to cause *Feather's Edge* to roll.

"Feather, Number two engine failure drill?" Sam prompted as she added rudder input to stop the yaw.

"Command Phantom Two is down. I say again, Phantom Two is down. I have visuals on both shoots," Telos called.

That seemed to snap Feather back into action, and the number two engine spun back to life.

"Check that, choppers are on their way."

"You alright to fly, Feather?" Sam asked. Feather nodded. "You want any checklists?"

There was no response from Feather.

"Phantom One and Three return for a visual landing," the controller instructed.

"Phantom One," Telos acknowledged for the formation.

"*Feather's Edge*, what is your altitude?"

"12,000 feet," Sam answered.

"Proceed for runway two-six. Expect number three for the visual approach."

"Expect visual two-six, and Western Air Command, can you let operations know we had some engine troubles?"

"Affirmative, do you wish to declare?"

"Negative, it's running fine now," Sam answered as Feather guided the aircraft towards the base.

"Greaser?" Flint called.

"Yes?"

"Is she going to be okay?"

"I don't know," Sam answered.

Patrick Gloutney

WCN *Stanton*

Vincent looked out over the water towards the *Lancer*. He couldn't imagine the stress its maintenance crew was under. At least he knew he could fix the *Stanton*. They were stuck with a ship that would need an entire electrical overhaul before it could sail under its own power again. Vincent shook his head and looked up to the blue fins on the main mast, where black smoke was now streaming out. They had managed to get both engines running again, though the left engine wasn't burning as clean as he would have liked. Nonetheless, they were no longer dead in the water. He was supposed to be bringing a report to the captain, but he found himself stalling. He had used only a small part of the *Stanton's* experimental armament in the last attack; even then, he knew there would be questions. Questions he wasn't sure he wanted to answer. There were consequences to that kind of firepower, and Vincent hoped the crew never realized just how severe those consequences could be. Now with both engines running, they could use each weapon to its full terrifying potential.

"Penny for your thoughts, Mr. Travis?" the captain's voice asked behind him.

Vincent jumped in surprise but handed his report to Delmar. "Both engines are operable. Hull repairs are holding. Other repairs were made, and they are detailed in the report."

Delmar nodded, accepting the report and looking out over the sea, "A pity, isn't it?"

"Sir?"

"Billions of dollars of government development, eighty crew, all gone in minutes," Delmar explained, "The *Juliane* never stood a chance."

Vincent chewed on his cheek; no one would stand a chance if the *Stanton* was forced to use its most lethal weapon.

"Did you know we switched positions with the *Juliane* just before the attack?" Delmar asked.

Vincent shook his head, "I was unaware, Sir."

Delmar shook his head, "I requested the change, with the jammed forward gun, I wanted it facing outside for the formation, not in. It could easily have been us sitting on the bottom of the sea."

Vincent sighed; he wasn't about to tell the captain how close they had been. The hull breaches, while minor, had been numerous. Had they joined together, the *Stanton* wouldn't have been afloat long.

"I thought those weapons weren't on the auxiliary system?"

Vincent tensed, "I got to thinking after our last conversation. I found one that drew less power, and it was able to be converted."

"And that was safe?" Delmar asked.

Vincent grimaced, "With all due respect, you know the answer to that."

Delmar nodded and sighed, leaning on the railing, "Command doesn't know who attacked us. Could be any number of governments that don't want this meeting to happen. I do know they will be back, though."

"Why not get the diplomats on board the *Stanton* and carry on?" Vincent suggested, "Maybe we can get out of bombing range."

Delmar smiled, "I've explored that possibility. They know something I don't about this ship as they refuse to come on board."

Vincent nodded, not too surprised. The tragedy that befell the *Stantons'* well-intentioned crew was classified, but anyone high enough in the government knew about it. "I can understand that."

Delmar eyed Vincent for a moment, "Knowing what you know, why are you here?"

Vincent arched an eyebrow, "Orders, Sir."

Delmar shook his head, "You could have resigned your commission. I'm sure you could have gotten an honourable discharge or at least reassigned to a different ship. Yet you chose to stay on board."

Vincent leaned on the railing with a sigh. Memories of his time on the *Stanton* washed over him: the victories, the losses, the long deployments, the people, and most pressing, the deaths. He could see the bodies of those who hadn't been vaporized scattered across the deck when their most powerful weapon had been discharged incorrectly during the heat of battle. Some were half-burned, others were melting. Vincent could still remember the smell and finding her.

Vincent shook his head to dispel the memories. He saw the captain still expecting an answer, "To protect everyone else."

"Protect us?" Delmar asked.

"The *Stanton* was often sent on long deployments. The crew became family to me. After the accident..." Vincent took a deep breath. "Some of these weapons never should have been built. I had to make sure they were used properly. Before someone like you comes along and history repeats itself."

Delmar said nothing before placing a hand on Vincent's shoulder, "I can't imagine what you've seen, but I thank you for being on board today. You've given us a chance."

Vincent shook his head, "Don't thank me till we make it home."

"They will be back. Whoever is after us won't give up that easily," Delmar remarked, "Do what you must to protect the ship." With that, the captain left. Vincent stayed, watching the *Lancer* move in the waves.

Patrick Gloutney

Protect the ship, he thought to himself, *but at what cost?*

Western Council Aerial Test Base

"Do you think it was maintenance?" Gypsy asked Telos as Sam and Feather entered the waiting room of the base's medical ward.

Telos sighed, "I don't think it was negligence if that's what you're asking."

Gypsy ran a hand through his hair, "It had to be the flight computer."

"They fixed that, in all of them," Telos said as Sam sat Feather down. Feather had been unsettlingly quiet after they landed. She hadn't spoken at all except to ask when she could go check in on Strafer. It got to the point where Boudreaux had decided to end the debrief until she could get her head on straight.

"His was the most problematic," Gypsy countered.

"What was wrong with the flight computers?" Feather asked.

Telos and Gypsy seemed to both be startled by Feather's question. Sam eyed them carefully. Gypsy was obviously the more rattled, but even Telos, who seemed usually stoic, looked upset by the turn of events.

Gypsy looked to Telos, who shrugged, "Initially, we had issues with the flight computer not responding to control inputs. It was caught on the ground, but now and again, we'd get sloppy control response in the air."

"Strafer's plane was particularly problematic," Telos elaborated, "But normally only if he rolled inverted. Last maintenance inspection, they found some problems, so he was limited not to doing that."

"But he did," Gypsy countered.

Telos turned to Gypsy, "He may not be the best pilot we have, but he's not stupid."

"Telos, I saw him roll inverted."

Telos rubbed his forehead, "There are only two people who know what happened to that jet. We just have to wait to talk with them." The room lapsed into silence. After a few moments, Feather spoke up.

"They both made it out. Right Telos?"

Telos looked up at her, "Yes, Claire. They both made it out. I don't know what shape they are in, though."

"Where's the rest of your crew?" Sam asked, noticing it was only Telos and Gypsy present.

"*W.S.O.* are helping with the planes. The remaining two aircraft have been grounded until further notice, so we were allowed to come here."

Sam noticed Feather start to anxiously tap on her knee, "Has he ever ejected before?"

"Jayhawk has, Strafer hasn't," Gypsy answered. Just then, Jayhawk was led into the waiting room. He walked over to the group, and Gypsy grabbed him in a hug. "How yah feeling man?"

Jayhawk was released from the hug and nodded to Telos, "Shaken but fine. No worse than when I ejected with you."

Telos grunted, "You have any idea what happened?"

Jayhawk shook his head, "We were trailing *Feather's Edge* just as they shot into their climb. Strafer said something about hitting their wake."

"Damn it," Telos muttered, "I was worried about that." Wake vortices were dangerous swirling air currents that extended horizontally behind the wings of an aircraft. If a small aircraft got caught in one, it could roll them right over. They were something that pilots are trained to avoid. Sam sighed. What was worse was the vortices produced by helicopters. And when they had pulled that climb, they had transitioned into a helicopter.

"When we rolled through inverted, we started diving. I guess the control system failed because he had me restart it, but by that time..."

"You were already too low," Telos muttered.

"We lost control at the end just before we punched out, too," Jayhawk explained.

"Explains why he would roll inverted," Gypsy commented.

"How is Tyler?" Feather asked from her seat.

Sam could see just how worried she was. *Geeze, how attached are you?*

"They are keeping him for observation overnight," Jayhawk stated, clearly dodging the question.

"Why? Is he hurt?" Feather asked.

Jayhawk shook his head, "Not really, no—"

"Can I see him?" Feather pushed.

"Feather," Sam interrupted, "Jayhawk doesn't have all the answers."

"Then who does?" Feather shot back, getting to her feet. Before Sam could react, Feather had barged through the doors leading to the medical ward.

"Um, Greaser...?" Flint began.

For the love of God, Sam thought to herself. "I'm on it."

WCN *Stanton*

"I don't like him," LeCroix stated as he stood beside Delmar on the catwalk as the sun set on the horizon.

"Why not?" Delmar asked, scanning the horizon with his binoculars.

"He has no respect for authority," LeCroix remarked, "And always thinks he knows more than anyone else on board."

Delmar laughed and lowered his binoculars, "That's because he does LeCroix."

LeCroix grumbled something under his breath.

"How long have you been an Executive Officer?"

"Quite a few years," LeCroix answered.

Delmar nodded, "Ever consider being a Captain?"

"Yes, Sir," LeCroix responded, "Navy just hasn't given me the chance yet."

"Think you have what it takes to command a ship?"

LeCroix seemed to shift beside him, "I believe so, Sir."

"What do you think makes a good Captain, LeCroix?" Delmar asked, turning to face his Executive Officer.

LeCroix arched an eyebrow, "Strong, assertive, intelligent—"

"Attributes to strive for, maybe," Delmar interrupted. "Let me ask you. Is a good Captain one who always knows what to do? He barks out orders left, right and center from his chair, needing no input from anyone. Just an unapproachable figure that will lead the ship and crew to victory, incapable of making mistakes?"

"Sounds about right for the Captains I've sailed with," LeCroix remarked, "It's what I've always tried to emulate."

Delmar nodded with a small smile, "Do you trust me to sail the *Stanton?*"

This seemed to throw LeCroix off. "Of course, Sir."

"Why?" Delmar asked.

"Why wouldn't I?" LeCroix asked, "You're our Captain."

"Yes," Delmar stated before motioning to the superstructure, "Yet my decisions disabled us for two days. You've just said a good Captain must be infallible. Does that mean I am not a good Captain LeCroix?"

"I...uhm..." LeCroix fumbled.

"There are many things that make a good Captain LeCroix. One of them is resource management," Delmar explained, "Mr. Travis is a very valuable resource to us, given how little we know about this ship. As Captain, I would have to be a fool not to give him liberty to best defend this ship. Does that make sense?"

LeCroix nodded, "Yes, Sir."

"Good," Delmar said, going back to scanning the horizon, "Best keep that in mind next time you are talking to Mr. Travis."

"Captain!" Someone called from the bridge, "New Airborne contact bearing two-seven-zero. Closing fast."

"Battle stations," Delmar ordered as he rushed inside, only to be greeted with a very unwelcome message.

"It's a missile Sir!"

So much for the EMP, Delmar thought, "All head full. Time to impact?"

"Thirty seconds Sir."

Delmar cursed under his breath, "Advise Mr. Travis. Ready counter-measures." He then brought his binoculars up. Sure enough, he could just make out the speck that was the missile heading for them.

"Missile impact in twenty seconds."

"Countermeasures ready, Sir," LeCroix advised.

Delmar nodded as the *Stanton* crashed through a wave. "Deploy counter-measures."

"Countermeasure away. Impact in ten," LeCroix advised.

"Attention all crew, brace for rapid repositioning," the computer called.

Rapid repositioning? Delmar asked himself.

"Nine, eight, seven, six," LeCroix continued counting down. "Counter-measure had no effect."

"Threat acquired," the computer advised.

"Four, three..."

"Aft thrusters active," the computer advised before the ship's stern was thrown to the side. Delmar just caught himself before he hit the floor. The ship spun 90 degrees around the bow as what looked like rockets on the side of the hull pushed the stern around seconds before impact. The sudden movement of the *Stanton* made it so the missile flew right past them, detonating a safe distance away.

Delmar wasted no time, "There will be more. Suggestions on protecting the *Oscoda,* Mr. Travis?"

"Position the *Stanton* between them and the missile."

"Sir, you can't possibly—" LeCroix protested.

"Two new missile contacts, bearing now zero-four-zero."

"How far apart, Mr. Travis?" Delmar asked over the intercom.

"At least 500 feet."

"LeCroix, take us into position," Delmar ordered.

LeCroix hesitated but soon started directing them into position.

"Impact in thirty seconds," he advised.

"Warning. Weapons discharge imminent. All hands below decks," the computer called as an alarm sounded through the bridge. Two metal beams extended from the side of the *Stanton* below the gunwale. The beams rotated before extending into what looked like an array of solar panels.

"Impact in fifteen seconds, Sir!" LeCroix shouted, "We need to move Captain."

"Anytime now, Mr. Travis," Delmar urged as he watched the missile speed straight towards them. Electricity seemed to spark across the newly extended panels. Seconds later, the missile exploded. Delmar wasn't able to keep his footing. The *Stanton* was once again thrown to the side towards the *Oscoda*. They came to rest less than 100 feet from the transport vessel.

Delmar got to his feet and looked back out. *Shields,* he thought in astonishment, *it has shields!* Sure enough, a semi-translucent wall extended from the panels forming a dome that covered the port side of the *Stanton,* and by positioning themselves where they had the shields had taken the impact for both the *Stanton* and the *Oscoda.*

"Sir, the Lancer!" LeCroix called. Delmar turned to see the *Lancer* listing in the water. Fire billowed from a hole in its stern.

"Any new contacts?" Delmar asked.

"Negative, Sir."

Delmar looked to the *Lancer* and then to the *Oscoda.* He couldn't protect them both. "Hold position."

There was a silent acknowledgment from the bridge crew. Delmar ran a hand through his hair. The *Oscoda* was the mission. The *Lancer* would evacuate if needed. They could pick up the lifeboats after. He just hoped the fires stayed away from the fuel and weapons holds.

The forward gunwales rose on the *Stanton* once again, the weapon from before extending forward.

"Can we see its targeting?" Delmar asked.

"Affirmative, it's targeting the origin of the missiles."

The shield deactivated as the forward weapon fired, the recoil sending the ship backward once again. Minutes passed as they waited for another attack or some sign that they were safe.

"Target destroyed, Sir," LeCroix reported. Delmar let out a sigh of relief as the weapons began to retract back into the *Stanton's* hull.

"Weapons Clear," the computer called.

"Radar, stay vigilant for additional targets. LeCroix, reposition us to help the *Lancer.*" No one had a chance to act on Delmar's order as the Lancer exploded. The blast decimated the wounded vessel.

Patrick Gloutney

Western Council Aerial Test Base

Tyler stared up at the ceiling, mulling over the crash. He shouldn't have let his position deteriorate the way it had. He had tried to reason that it was a fluke, but one fact remained. Telos hadn't hit the wake the same way. He had avoided it just like Tyler should have.

"Tyler?" a soft voice asked from the doorway, "You awake?"

Tyler contemplated faking being asleep. He wasn't sure he was ready to face anyone yet. He let out a sigh. He couldn't lie to Claire, "Yes, Claire."

He felt her hand on his. "How are you feeling?"

"Like I got my ass kicked, "Sorry to ruin the war game."

Claire let out a sad laugh and shook her head, "I'm just glad you're alright." They remained silent, with Claire just holding his hand as all the things he should have done ran through Tyler's head. He should have reacted quicker when his Phantom started rolling, and pulled up faster, to hell with potential airframe damage from the Gs. It would have been better than losing the aircraft.

"Stop," Claire said, gently caressing his cheek with her hand, "You got unlucky. It's not your fault."

Tyler looked into her eyes and sighed, "Easy for you to say."

"It doesn't help," Claire reasoned. "You're talking to the pilot who made the wake that nearly killed you."

"Telos—"

"Agrees it was likely system failure, not pilot error," Claire interrupted.

Tyler sighed and reached up to grab her free hand. "Thank you."

Claire smiled, "For what?"

"Being here," Tyler answered and smiled as Claire ducked her head, blushing.

"Even when she's not supposed to be here," Greaser's voice called from the doorway. Tyler arched an eyebrow, only for Claire to smile sheepishly. "How are you feeling, Strafer?"

"Better now," Tyler answered, still holding Claire's hand.

"Good," Greaser remarked. "Feather, we are supposed to be at a briefing."

"I just wanted to see him," Claire argued.

"I know," Greaser said with a smile, "but you need to be at this briefing."

"Go," Tyler encouraged. "I will be here when you get back. Promise."

Claire nodded and leaned forward to kiss Tyler on the forehead, "Love you."

"Love you too," Tyler said with a smile, feeling a weight lift off his chest at finally saying those words. Greaser shook her head and herded the smiling Claire out of the room.

She paused before following her fellow pilot, "You should know why we are briefing."

"They're trying to lay blame?" Tyler asked.

Greaser shook her head, "The remaining Phantoms and *Feather's Edge* are being deployed within the week."

WCN *Stanton*

The drone of the Stanton's engines filled the air as Vincent leaned against a support column in the engine room. He took a deep breath; the scent of grease and diesel fumes filled his nose as his eyes drifted and then closed. The *Stanton* had managed to save the *Oscoda,* but it had cost them the *Lancer.* Thankfully, some of the *Lancer's* crew had been saved from the burning wreck. The attack had also exposed what Vincent had assumed about some of the weapons on board. Not all of them were functioning properly. The shields were not only supposed to stop attacks but also absorb the impact. The movement of the *Stanton* after the missile impact showed that it hadn't happened. Something else he had to add to his list of repairs that were needed.

Someone shaking his shoulder pulled him from his thoughts. He was greeted by the worried face of Harris. Harris motioned for Vincent to follow out of the main engine room. Vincent nodded; they'd have a hard time talking over the engine noise anyway.

"You look like hell, man," Harris remarked as they entered the control room.

Vincent waved him off, "I'm fine."

"Vincent, I just found you asleep next to a running engine," Harris protested, "When's the last time you slept?"

Vincent shrugged, "It wasn't that long ago. I got an hour or two last night."

Harris crossed his arms. "When was the last time you got a proper sleep?"

Vincent shook his head. "I'm fine."

"You have been here every day I have reported to duty, and when I leave. The point of having an Assistant Chief Engineer is so you don't have to do it all," Harris argued, "Have you even slept since the first attack?"

"A few hours," Vincent answered, though he knew it was likely an hour, at most, a night. He had been so busy making sure the repairs were progressing and prepping the weapons in case they were needed.

"Vincent, man, it's been four days. Go get some sleep. I'll get you if we need anything." Vincent was about to protest when Harris continued, "You are no use tired. What if you fire the wrong weapon? Or fall asleep when we need you?"

Vincent sighed; Harris was right. "Fine. You call the second something goes wrong, though."

"Yes, boss," Harris agreed.

"And don't let anyone touch the shield generators. We need to—"

"No one is touching any of that stuff without you around," Harris interrupted, "We are all too worried about blowing ourselves out of the water."

Vincent nodded. As he was about to leave, he stopped and turned back, "Harris? Thanks."

Harris smiled, "Anytime, boss."

Vincent nodded and stepped out into the corridor. He only made it halfway to his bunk when he ran into LeCroix and a couple of crew members whom Vincent didn't recognize.

"Mr. Travis," LeCroix said as they approached, "Can we have a moment?" Vincent fought back a yawn and nodded. "These men are from the *Lancer*. They were hoping to ask you about the way we fought in the last attack."

"Sir, with all due respect, I am exhausted. Can this wait till later?" Vincent asked.

LeCroix arched an eyebrow, "These men just lost their ship and many friends. Surely you can spare a moment to help them get closure."

Nice guilt trip, Vincent thought to himself, "Very well, Sir. What do they wish to know?"

"Why weren't we made aware of the *Stantons'* capabilities?" one of the men asked.

"You're asking the wrong person. I don't know." Vincent answered.

"Where were you in the first attack?" another of the men asked bluntly.

Vincent glanced at LeCroix, taken aback by how direct the *Lancer* crew was, "In the engine room."

"Don't play coy. Why wasn't the battle group defended by the *Stanton?*"

"We weren't authorized to discharge any of our...unique armament," Vincent responded calmly.

"What changed?" the first man asked.

"We got authorization to protect everyone with our full armament."

"Didn't do a very good job of that," a third man remarked.

"Why didn't you just make a big shield around everyone?" the first man pushed.

Vincent cocked his head to the side, "The shield generators aren't designed for that. What is this really about?"

"Why were we left defenceless?" the second member of the *Lancer's* crew asked.

"I can't answer that," Vincent stated cautiously as he noted how agitated the men seemed to be getting. He looked to LeCroix for help but found none. "Captain Delmar ultimately directs the actions of this ship. I just follow my orders."

"That's not entirely true, Mr. Travis," LeCroix stated, "It was you who directed the captain to position the *Stanton* between the missile and the *Oscoda.*"

"You son of a bitch," the third *Lancer* crewmember said grabbing Vincent and slamming him against the wall.

"I was ordered—" Vincent protested.

"To protect the escort group," LeCroix stated.

Vincent shot him a confused glare, "No—"

"What about us!" the man holding Vincent shouted, "Brothers in arms, left for dead." A fist slammed into Vincent's chin before the man dropped him to the floor.

"While you sit safe and protected," the man seethed, his crewmembers joining in as he kicked Vincent in the side. Vincent doubled over in pain before a second kick hit his gut.

"We could only defend one," Vincent coughed out, "The *Oscoda* was...the logical choice."

Vincent was pulled to his feet by the collar of his uniform. "You chose wrong," the man growled before punching Vincent once again across the face and dropping him. Vincent bashed his head against the bulkhead. He barely registered the shouting and further beating as he blacked out.

Western Council Aerial Test Base

Sam scanned over the file in front of her. A lot of it had been redacted, but what was available to them was scary, to say the least.

"They aren't ready for deployment," Telos protested from across the table. He and General Reed had been arguing back and forth about the suitability of the *Phantoms* for this assignment.

"They have to be. It's the only way," Reed explained.

"Why not load them on the...*Stanton*," Sam suggested, "It's reported as serviceable."

Reed sighed, "The intricacies of this operation are not up for discussion. You are being ordered to deploy."

"Sir," Telos continued, "With all due respect, we just lost a *Phantom* due to a flight computer failure. You can't possibly think it's a good idea to push these aircraft after that."

"Was that *Phantom* not prone to that failure?"

"Yes," Telos conceded.

"And your pilot violated a maintenance restriction by rolling inverted, did he not?"

No one refuted the argument. Even though it hadn't been Strafer's fault, the fact remained that Reed was right. It wouldn't have happened if they hadn't been flipped by the wake turbulence.

"Why us, though?" Gypsy asked again, "What makes it so you can't just send anything else?"

Reed drummed his fingers on the table and nodded, "The escort group was hit with an Electro-Magnetic Pulse during the first attack. You are all we have in our arsenal that can withstand such an attack."

Sam glanced at Feather, noticing she was biting her nails and grimacing. She sighed; they were likely retrofitting the aircraft right now. "How are we going to deal with the difference between the aircraft types?"

Reed arched an eyebrow, "*Feather's Edge* was designed for joint combat missions like this."

"Not without first thinking it through," Sam protested, "We are still a prop and they are a jet. They need to cruise higher to be efficient, and their endurance is shorter than ours."

Reed nodded, "That's for you all to coordinate. You will launch off a carrier as close as possible to the target. It will be well within range." With that, he took his leave.

Sam shook her head, leaning back in her chair.

"This is bull shit," Gypsy said finally.

"He's only hearing what he wants to hear," Telos agreed.

"Nonetheless, we have to make this work," Sam argued, "If he's right, we are the only chance of getting them out of there."

"You're not flying a death trap," Gypsy shot back.

Sam shook her head and turned to *Feather*. She hadn't been the same since the accident, and Sam worried about her ability to continue flying *Feather's Edge*. "Any ideas, Feather?"

Feather looked up, seeming to snap out of her daze, "Sorry?"

"Great, just great," Gypsy remarked.

"Delay their departure," Feather spoke.

"Pardon?" Telos asked.

"We leave first from the carrier. The *Phantoms* cruise faster than us at altitude, they can catch up. Just time it right and it solves a lot of the compatibility issues."

Telos nodded, "That leaves you unprotected."

"We have advanced stealth technology," Sam responded, "It's unlikely they would catch us on the radar. It could work."

"Plus, I don't think they need much protection," Gypsy remarked, "if the last two tests are any indication."

Feather shook her head, "We still need protection. We will be vulnerable when loading the diplomats."

"We will run a perimeter patrol and intercept anything that comes up," Telos stated, "Not quite what we were designed, for but it will work."

"We need practice runs. Lots of them," Gypsy remarked.

"We can make arrangements," Telos responded. "Let's get to it shall we?"

Everyone stood up and filed out of the room except Sam. She glanced through the file again. Something felt off.

"You think it too, don't you?" Telos asked from the door.

"Think what?" Sam asked, getting up.

"That they aren't telling us the whole truth."

Patrick Gloutney

WCN *Stanton*

Delmar sat on his bunk, looking at his Executive Officer in disbelief, "He fell down the stairs?"

"So, it appears, Sir," LeCroix answered.

"Who found him?" Delmar asked.

"Assistant Chief Mechanic Harris, Sir."

Delmar stood up, twirling a pen between his fingers, "Was this before or after you brought the *Lancer* crew to see him?"

"After I left, though, shortly after the introductions," LeCroix explained.

Delmar shook his head. He looked out the porthole in his quarters. The rain was beginning to fall, and the swells were getting heavier. If the ship's weather radar was to be believed, there was a nice storm coming their way over the next day or two.

How does an experienced sailor fall down a set of stairs? Delmar asked himself, "You realize this puts us at a significant disadvantage."

"Yes, Sir."

Delmar nodded and put down the pen, "I don't like it. I don't like it one bit. I want guards protecting Mr. Travis while he recovers. Let's hope that this storm buys us some time."

"I can work with Travis to learn the weapons system once he has recovered enough," LeCroix offered.

Delmar nodded but then stopped, "We will cross that bridge when we get to it. Dismissed."

With that, LeCroix took his leave. Delmar looked back out of his porthole. Something didn't sit right with this whole situation. Delmar sighed and walked out to the hallway. Stepping out on the deck in the rain, moments later, he looked along the *Stantons'* hull. He noted that one of the panels that must have hidden the shield generators hadn't retracted properly and was slightly ajar. A reminder that while the *Stanton* was holding its own now, there was no telling how long she'd last.

Delmar looked out to the *Oscoda* rocking in the waves. While the storm would likely save them from further attacks and give them time to make repairs, he worried about the *Oscoda*'s ability to weather it. Without their propulsion, it would be at the mercy of the sea.

Those reinforcements can't get here fast enough, Delmar thought. On his way back inside, something caught his eye. The fins on the main mast seemed to have streaks of blue light flickering through them. Puzzled, Delmar walked closer to it. Delmar didn't know enough about the weapons on board to know what he was looking at, but from talking with Vincent, he could gather that the weapons they were carrying should be treated with a healthy amount of apprehension. He watched as the blue light flickered a few more times before the fins went dark again.

Delmar shook his head and made his way below decks to the engine room. On arrival, he found Harris hunched over an instrument panel.

"Everything alright, Mr. Harris?"

Harris turned towards Delmar with a start, "Sir, I wasn't made aware—"

Delmar waved him off, "It's just a visit, Mr. Harris. What had you so engrossed?"

Harris stepped aside, "Nothing major, just some unexplained spikes in the power draw off the generators."

Delmar surveyed the panel and noticed that a few gauges were jumping erratically. "Any ideas what is causing it?"

Harris shook his head, "It's happened before. Travis usually took care of it."

Delmar nodded, "Did he train you at all on the weapons system?"

Harris grimaced, "When we had time, yes. But honestly, we've been so busy with repairs that I don't know enough about him to feel I was safe."

Delmar sighed, "It may have to do. I noticed the fins on the mast had light running through them. Could that be the draw?"

Harris shrugged, "Maybe, I don't even know what those are for."

Delmar sighed, "Any word on his condition?"

Harris shook his head, "No, Sir."

"I must admit I wasn't paying that close attention to him. How was he leading up to all this?" Delmar inquired.

"He was stressed and tired. He's been working himself to the bone. We all have been," Harris answered.

Delmar sighed; he had taken Vincent for granted. "And how are you holding up?"

"Sir?"

"You found your chief unconscious after falling down a set of stairs. I can't imagine that was easy," Delmar remarked.

Harris raised an eyebrow, "Fell downstairs?"

Please don't say what I think you are about to say, Delmar prayed.

"Sir, Vincent didn't fall. He was beaten."

Patrick Gloutney

WCN *Stanton*

The deck heaved in the large swells as the storm battered the ship. Every time the bow slammed into a wave; Delmar winced. His concerns over their weakened hull grew with the groans of the ship. The storm had picked up overnight, and with massive swells throwing the ship around, he had suspended all non-essential duty. His thoughts turned to Vincent Travis. A quick visit to the Naval Surgeon had confirmed what Harris told him. Travis had been beaten. The injuries weren't enough to kill him, but it would make his service difficult while he recovered.

Can I even ask that of him? Delmar wondered. He needed that man on duty if they were to have any hope of protecting the *Oscoda* against further attacks. He also knew it would mean rushing him back into service. *Reduced duty, maybe.* Delmar glanced at LeCroix; he had yet to reveal to any of the crew the true nature of Travis's injuries, and he didn't want mass panic in an already stressful situation. He had confined the remaining Lancer survivors, having suspicions that they were responsible. He had other concerns, however, one look at Vincent had been enough for Delmar to think he had been attacked, so why hadn't LeCroix noticed that?

Panic? He asked himself as a crack of thunder rolled through the ship. Vincent was an important part of the crew, so his incapacitation was concerning, but LeCroix was an experienced Executive Officer who had seen combat before. Delmar shook his head; nothing about this sat well with him.

He looked out the windows into the storm. Flashes of lightning lit up the dark clouds as the rain pelted the ship. He could see the *Oscoda* struggling in the waves.

"Any reports on how the hull repairs are faring?" Delmar asked.

"The ones that have been inspected are holding for now," LeCroix reported.

"Our position?"

"Still drifting inland," LeCroix answered.

Delmar nodded; they had been following the drift of the *Oscoda,* but the storm had been pushing them closer toward land, in the same direction the bombers had come from. However, with the *Oscoda* dead in the water and the diplomat's refusal to transfer ships, they were left with no choice.

"I've got a problem, Sir," the radar operator called.

Delmar quickly made his way over to the sailor. "What kind of problem?"

"I don't know Sir." The radar console's display was flickering on and off making it almost impossible to read.

"It's happening here too, Sir," LeCroix remarked from another console. A loud crack of thunder sounded, and every display on the bridge started to malfunction.

What the hell is going on? Delmar asked himself before another loud crack of thunder shook the ship, and blue light erupted outside. An alarm sounded through the bridge, but they lost all electrical power to the bridge before Delmar could figure out what it was signalling.

"LeCroix report," Delmar ordered as he looked at the water surrounding them. Icy blue lightning seemed to arc from the ship to the water sporadically.

The emergency lights snapped on as LeCoix answered, "Main power's down. Back-up systems coming online."

"Another attack?" Delmar asked.

"I don't think so Sir," LeCroix answered. Then the fire alarm rang out. Delmar looked to LeCroix, who was already looking at the ship's status panel. LeCroix paused and looked up to Delmar with concern evident in his eyes, "There's a fire in the engine room."

Patrick Gloutney

WCN *Stanton*

Harris and the other mechanics all watched the instruments with puzzled expressions. The needles on the electrical systems gauges were bouncing erratically while the engines seemed to rev up higher.

"Any ideas?" Someone asked. Harris shook his head. "Should we get Travis?"

"I don't want to drag him down here over a power surge," Harris refused.

"It's not like any power surge I've seen before."

"Warning," the computer called, "Excessive weapons power draw." With that, the amperage and load gauges pegged themselves past the red line on both generator systems.

Harris swallowed as the RPM on the port engine began to rev past the red line, "I take it back. Get Travis. Now." They never had the chance, however, as an alarm sounded throughout the engine room, followed by an eruption of sparks.

Harris shielded his eyes as the engine screamed louder. Then the fire alarm sounded. He jumped to his feet. "Fire on the port generator!"

Harris rushed down the stairs leading to the main floor. He stopped when he saw a bolt of electricity arc through the air and strike the ceiling.

He turned back, "It's too dangerous, shut it down."

"There were men in there, Sir," someone remarked.

Harris clenched his fists. *Why isn't the fire suppression system active?*

"Shut it down, then we can look for the injured," Harris ordered. The sailors rushed to comply. Harris walked to the fire suppression panel to find it hadn't activated as intended. He shook his head and began the manual activation. He threw the activation switch only for it to smoke, and a fault light to illuminate.

Thanks, Stanton, he grimaced. He heard the port engine spool down to a stop and looked out to see some injured men trying to make their way to the control room. He grabbed a fire extinguisher and rushed out, with others behind him. The others helped the injured while Harris tried to keep the fire away from their still-running engine. It was no use; he quickly depleted the fire extinguisher, tossing it aside.

"Everyone out now!" he ordered, helping people up the stairs. The heat of the fires was making it almost unbearable to stand in the engine room. Harris looked around, fire lapping at the damaged generator, inching its way toward the starboard engine and the fuel lines.

"Harris!" he heard Vincent call, "In here now!"

Harris didn't hesitate; he found Vincent at the fire suppression panel, grunting, trying to pry the panel open. "Open it," he ordered.

Harris grabbed the pry bar and pulled the panel open. He watched as Vincent grabbed a wrench. "You can fix it?"

"No time," Vincent responded, wrapping a strip of rubber around his hand before jamming the wrench in the panel. It sparked and smoked before a tone sounded.

"Fire suppression and containment are active. Evacuate," the computer called. Harris helped Vincent to his feet, and they joined the others outside in the hallway as containment walls sealed off the port engine and generator.

Once the watertight door was sealed, Vincent and Harris collapsed on the floor. "You...You alright, Vincent?"

Vincent nodded, panting, "Peachy." He grunted in discomfort before chuckling, "So I leave my engine room in your hands for a day and what? You try to blow it up?"

Harris chuckled, "Fuck man, we are lucky to have you."

"Make a hole!" Delmar's voice called as he and LeCroix charged down the hall. "Vincent?"

"Fire is contained, Sir," Vincent answered.

"All men accounted for," Harris added.

Delmar nodded, "Good work then. LeCroix see to it that the wounded are tended to."

LeCroix nodded, "Good to see you back, Mr. Travis."

"Yeah," Vincent said, Harris could just catch the uneasy tone in his voice, "I'm sure you are."

Feather's Edge

"Phantoms in position," Telos radioed. Sam glanced out her window to visually confirm that the Phantoms were in position, flanking *Feather's Edge*.

"Confirmed," she called.

"Confirmed," Feather reported.

"All units ready to engage?" Command asked. Sam acknowledged them.

"Systems check?" Feather asked.

"All green. No limitations," Sam answered.

"Ready for this?" Flint asked. Sam and Feather nodded. They were running a simulated rescue attempt of the diplomats by using a target in the desert. They would fly with the Phantoms initially, trying to make it difficult for radar to identify them, if it could pick the formation of stealth aircraft at all.

"Game's hot. Have fun," Command advised. With that, Feather led the formation to the lowest altitude they were allowed. Due to concerns over the Phantoms' flight controls, they remained above 10,000 ft. At least until they broke off the formation when Feather would descend to the target.

"Contact bearing three-six-zero twenty miles," Flint reported.

"Hold formation," Feather ordered, "Sam, I want you ready on the speed brakes."

"Armed," Sam answered as she moved the control into position, even though it was not quite the right phase of flight for that command. As much as they had standard operating procedures, it was often better to follow Feather when she went off script. She had more information than Sam did.

"Contact's now ten miles out," Flint reported.

"Phantoms, you have the targets?" Sam asked.

"Affirmative," Telos responded.

"They are all yours. Break!" Feather ordered as she brought the throttles to idle. The Phantoms shot ahead of them as *Feather's Edge* rolled onto its back before tucking into a nosedive. "Speed brakes full."

"Selected," Sam called, pulling the lever back as they dove. The extra drag from the brakes prevented them from overspeeding the airframe.

As they neared the ground, Feather called as she manipulated the controls, "Engines 45 degrees." Sam felt the Gs push her into her seat as they pulled out of the dive. She grunted in discomfort as the aircraft levelled off before speeding along the desert floor.

"Engines zero, Speed breaks zero," Feather ordered.

"Selected," Sam answered. Feather pushed their aircraft as low as they were allowed towards their target. Sam scanned their instruments, looking for anything out of place. As per usual, Feather was flying *Feather's Edge* exactly to spec.

"30 seconds to target," Sam called out.

"Prepare for loading," Feather ordered.

"On it," Flint responded. This next part was the hardest for them. Flint had to leave her station to load the diplomats. It would leave Sam and Feather one set of eyes short to operate *Feather's Edge*. It would mean limited threat information while they held the hover to load. If there was a time they were going to get shot down, it was then, when Feather's hands were tied in terms of maneuverability.

Feather banked steeply around the target, bleeding off their speed before pulling into a hover. "Stable."

"Doors coming down," Flint called as the wind and engine noise flooded the aircraft with the lowering of the rear cargo ramp.

"Starting timer," Sam called. They had estimated five minutes to load the diplomats, so during that time, it was up to the *Phantoms* to keep them safe. The problem was, as far as Sam was aware, the Phantoms were busy with the enemy aircraft they had found earlier.

"We're sitting ducks," Feather stated the obvious, tapping her fingers on the throttles, "Call the Phantoms back closer to us."

"*Feather's Edge* to Phantom One," Sam radioed.

"Kind of busy," Telos's voice called back.

Damn, Sam muttered, turning her attention to her threat display before turning back to the aircraft's instruments. It was an odd division of attention for her, and she was worried she'd mismanaged the balance. Seconds ticked by as Feather held *Feather's Edge* in its hover. Then, with only 30 seconds left on the clock till they could move a missile lock tone sounded.

"Shit," Flint cursed.

Sam sighed and reached to queue her mic, "*Feather's Edge* is dead."

Patrick Gloutney

WCN *Stanton*

"Don't encourage him, Captain," the Naval Surgeon cautioned. He had just finished verbally lashing Vincent for returning to his station so soon. Vincent shook his head; he was sore, but nothing he couldn't deal with. "Don't shake your head at me, sailor; a fractured rib is nothing to ignore so carelessly."

With Vincent's nod of acknowledgment, the Naval Surgeon took his leave so that Vincent and Delmar had the room to themselves.

"Never a dull moment," Delmar remarked.

"A ship this old keeps you on your toes," Vincent answered, wincing as he readjusted his position. Perhaps he was a bit more than sore.

"You should have left the situation to those on duty," Delmar stressed.

Vincent shook his head, "And what, watch as we lost all propulsion again? Not after what it took to get us moving."

Delmar sighed, "Have you always been this stubborn, Mr. Travis?"

"Captain," Vincent stated, "With all due respect, you can save the leadership crap. We both know you need me on duty."

Delmar raised an eyebrow. "Your attitude has some officers worried."

"I don't blame them."

"How bad was the fire?"

Vincent rolled his neck, "The port generator is damaged but repairable. The port engine escaped serious damage. More concerning to me is the failure of the fire suppression and containment system. I've got Harris checking every safety system now."

Delmar nodded, "Any idea of the cause?"

"One of the weapons is breaking down. It's been drawing power since we left port when it's not supposed to be. I think the static from the storm caused it to surge, blowing out the generator. I've shown Harris how to prevent it from happening again," Vincent explained.

"You're right, Mr. Travis," Delmar stated, "I do need you on duty. But only what you are physically capable of. You are to coordinate repairs only for now. Is that clear?"

"Yes, Sir," Vincent answered.

Delmar was silent for a moment before he took a seat. "I also need to know who attacked you."

Vincent looked away. He knew Delmar would ask eventually, but he also knew he was testing his limits with not only the captain but also the other officers. "And if you don't like my answer?"

Delmar leaned forward in his chair. "What do you mean not like your answer?"

Something in Delmar's tone warned Vincent he was approaching dangerous waters: "Some of the *Lancer* crew."

Delmar nodded, "I figured. I've confined them for now to avoid a repeat. Any idea why they would target you?"

Vincent gritted his teeth. He knew if he told the captain that he suspected LeCroix, it would end badly. It always did for the assault victim. Memories of betrayal, blame, and accusations flitted through his mind.

"No, Sir." Better just to keep his mouth shut.

Delmar was silent for a moment before he sighed, "You really want to start lying to me?"

Vincent flinched, "I..." A glare from Delmar made Vincent relent, "They weren't happy with the *Lancer* being left undefended during the attacks. I guess they felt cheated."

Delmar arched an eyebrow, "That's not something to attack an engineer over."

Vincent nodded, "LeCroix may have..."

"May have what?" Delmar pushed.

Vincent chewed on his lip, "He spoke in a way that may have misled them to believe that I was responsible." Better to be as diplomatic as possible to avoid having it come back to bite him.

"You suggesting he prompted the attack?" Delmar asked. Vincent remained silent. "That's a grave accusation."

Vincent nodded, "I make no accusations, Sir."

Delmar's questioning eyes studied Vincent, causing the engineer to squirm. "Very well."

Vincent let out a sigh of relief; he then reached for a package of papers and handed them to Delmar, "As requested, a list of every weapon on board. I also included their limitations."

Delmar accepted the stack of papers. "That's quite the list."

"We are well equipped. But with a generator down, we have to be careful."

"How so?" Delmar asked, flipping through the package.

"Shields for one," Vincent explained. "They each need a dedicated generator, so right now you can only use one at a time. Some of the high-power energy weapons also need both generators. There's a page at the back detailing the impact of the lost generator."

Delmar nodded, "I see why you've been so hesitant with these."

Vincent sighed, "Learn that information backward and forward, Sir. One misstep and it can have disastrous consequences."

"We will discuss how to best work together with these," Delmar stated, "That way you can act as a check to stop me from making a misstep."

"There's one big limitation you need to know, Captain," Vincent pushed.

"And that is?"

"You cannot fire any weapons with the shield up. They are a wall on both sides, and deflect what hits them in the opposite direction," Vincent explained.

"So if we fire with them up..."

"It could mean the destruction of the *Stanton*."

Western Council Aerial Test Base

"We're clashing," Claire spoke up, interrupting Reed, who was explaining a new tactic to try for the next training mission. They had been flying attempt after attempt with the same results. *Feather's Edge* was always shot down while loading the diplomats.

"Pardon?" Reed asked, and all eyes turned to Claire. Tyler, who had been called into the mission to help consult on ways to improve their tactics, closed the folder in front of him, eager to hear Claire for the first time since he had arrived.

"We aren't working together. The Phantoms are off doing their own thing and we are doing ours," Claire explained, "It's the only reason we keep failing."

"Or you could pay attention to your threat displays," Gypsy grumbled. Tyler rolled his eyes.

"You could just protect us like you're supposed to," Flint shot back.

Gypsy laughed, "I'm sure you think it's that easy."

"Alright, guys just—" Sam tried, but Flint had to get the last word in.

"It was when we shot all three Phantoms down."

Gypsy stood up but Tyler put a hand on his shoulder, "Don't let your ego get away from you."

Gypsy glared at Tyler, "Let your girlfriends fight for themselves." Tyler flinched as he caught Reed raising an eyebrow.

"Enough," Telos interjected, "Gypsy, you are dismissed." Gypsy snarled but left nonetheless.

Telos sighed, "Forgive him, we've had to rewrite our entire playbook with the loss of Phantom Two. It's been rather stressful."

"We are both a man down. I don't have Flint watching my back either," Sam assured, "But Feather's right, we aren't working well as a team."

"Strafer, any thoughts?" Reed asked.

Tyler looked around the room before looking at the closed file folder in front of him. "Why so many enemy fighters? It almost seems like a no-win situation."

Reed leaned back in his chair. "It's our best guess on the worst-case scenario the rescue party may encounter."

Tyler nodded, "Feather, what's the main reason you are getting shot down?"

Feather cocked her head to the side, "Lack of protection while we are vulnerable."

"What about Flint?" Tyler asked.

"What about her?" Sam called back, an edge in her voice.

"If you had her back at her station, you might be able to better defend yourself, correct?"

Telos leaned forward. "Strafer, you just crashed a jet."

"I'm cleared to fly," Tyler pushed back. He saw a light turn on in Claire's eyes as she realized what he was getting at.

"You want to fly with us?" she asked excitedly.

Reed drummed his fingers on the table. "Adding one crew member will fix our problems?"

Tyler shook his head, "Not the working together part. But if I'm right, it will make *Feather's Edge* less reliant on the Phantom's protection while it's hovering."

Reed turned to Claire and Sam, "This true?"

Sam nodded hesitantly, "In theory, yes."

Reed smiled, "Excellent, make it happen."

Patrick Gloutney

WCN *Stanton*

Delmar scrolled through the *Stantons'* digital archive on his station in his quarters. His access gave him everything from historical crew logs to maintenance reports, though most of the information about the ship's armament was redacted. That information, however, was not what he was looking for. Something Mr. Travis had said worried him. Delmar didn't appreciate being lied to, but something about the way Travis's behaviour had shifted led him to believe that the man was hiding something. With tensions running high among all crews involved it was understandable that the *Lancer* crew was angry and could misinterpret LeCroix's description of Travis's role in the ship's operation. That said, Delmar couldn't shake the feeling that Travis believed LeCroix directed the attack, whether the engineer was willing to say it to him or not.

Regardless if it was true or not, the fact that Travis was reluctant to report his suspicions was a concern to Delmar. He wanted issues like this addressed without fear of retribution for the victim involved.

He took a sip from his coffee mug as he continued to scroll through, eventually finding what he was looking for: reprimands and investigation reports of past crew members. He searched Travis's name, and sure enough, a lengthy report came up.

"Son of a bitch," Delmar muttered as he read the report. This was not the first time Travis had been beaten. The report outlined at least three other instances in which Travis had been assaulted on board. What sickened Delmar was how one-sided the report seemed. It outlined Travis as a belligerent and insubordinate crew member. It downplayed the beatings as a form of disciplinary action and cited Travis as a martyr for his appeals to the investigation.

Delmar leaned back in his chair, rubbing the bridge of his nose. He had seen nothing to support the claims in the report; however, it shed light on Travis's behaviour. In the heat of the moment, he was very confident and independent, but he always seemed to be looking over his shoulder. Being the longest-serving member of the *Stanton,* his superiors must not have liked him knowing more about the ship than they, especially if their interactions had been like Delmar had first had with the man.

Delmar stood up to pace his quarters. *That's no excuse to beat a man,* he thought to himself. He felt sick knowing this could be going on, and the fact that the report had been reviewed by Command and reprimands had been issued. It meant they saw no issue with what was going on, despite the report clearly showing officers covering up unnecessarily brutal treatment of crewmembers. They were supposed to be the good guys in the war. The other countries abused their soldiers and their people. It was why the war had begun in the first place. Now, though, it seemed the Alliance was becoming hypocritical in the long-standing conflict.

This report also shed new light on LeCroix, mainly his belief that a Captain was to be infallible and not questioned, made a lot of sense if those asking the questions were beaten. It was an unhealthy ship environment that only led to disaster. Much to Delmar's dismay, it also meant that LeCroix could potentially believe in that method of leadership, and could mean he saw Travis much the way those who beat him in the past had: a threat to their Captain's command.

A knock sounded on the door. "Enter," Delmar called.

LeCroix stepped through the doorway. "There's a call for you on the Sat-Com. It's Whiteford herself."

Delmar arched an eyebrow, shutting off his monitor, "I'll take it on my secure line. You are dismissed." LeCroix nodded, and Delmar picked up his secure SatCom phone. "Ma'am?"

"Captain Delmar," Whiteford greeted, "What's the status of your ship?"

Things must be getting worse if she's calling, Delmar thought, "Repairs are underway. We estimate to have full systems in the next day or two."

"Good," Whiteford said. "I'll have an evac group on their way to you soon, but it will still take a few days to reach your location. Can you hold your position?"

Delmar shook his head, "The storm has drifted the *Oscoda* inland, and we've followed."

"Of course, it has," Whiteford sighed. "As soon as the evac flight has retrieved the diplomats I want you to haul ass home Captain."

"What of the mission, Ma'am?" Delmar asked.

"It is to be abandoned; your only priority is the safety of your crew."

Delmar nodded, then paused, "And the *Oscoda's* crew?"

There was a moment of silence before Whiteford responded, "You're on a secure line?"

"Yes, Ma'am. It's just you and me."

"We have all been tricked, Captain Delmar," Whiteford explained, "I'm sorry to say that this has been an ambush from the moment you set sail." Whiteford sighed, "I fear the *Oscoda* has been compromised. Treat its crew with suspicion when you bring them aboard."

"Understood, Ma'am."

"And Delmar," Whiteford spoke, "Be careful of whom you trust."

Patrick Gloutney

Western Council Aerial Test Base

Tasia Whiteford watched quietly through the video feeds as *Feather's Edge* held its hover over the target. In light of recent developments, she had decided to come to see the team's progress firsthand. With the two Phantom jets busy dealing with various assailants, two more fighters slipped in low level towards the vulnerable *Feather's Edge*. However, unlike the exercises she had watched in her office, *Feather's Edge* didn't stay still. It rotated around the target, so it was facing the oncoming threat before knocking them both out.

"That's more like it," Tasia stated. Beside her, Reed nodded as *Feather's Edge* finished loading before dipping low and speeding back toward base.

"Command, *Feather's Edge* is free and clear," Sam radioed. Tasia stepped back from the displays and made her way outside to watch them land. Reed soon joined her.

"I like this new approach," Tasia stated after a few moments. "I want them deployed by day's end."

Reed arched an eyebrow, "This is their only success. They aren't ready."

Tasia shook her head, "That's an order. We don't have time for more runs. I've stationed carriers along their route. They'll hop from ship to ship to reduce transport time."

"With all due respect, Ma'am," Reed pushed. "Surely one day won't hurt."

"You've seen the reports on the *Stanton,* haven't you?" Tasia answered. Reed nodded. "It's gotten worse. There was a fire on board yesterday, and it knocked out a bunch of their systems. I don't know how long they can hold out."

"Any injuries?" Reed asked.

Tasia shook her head, "Not that I was briefed on, but morale on that ship must be plummeting. We need to get there before they give up entirely."

"Ma'am, if I may, why don't you order the diplomats onto the *Stanton* and avoid this whole mess?"

Tasia drummed her fingers on the railing before her as *Feather's Edge* flew overhead, pulling into a victory roll. She had debated that order herself, but given the nature of the *Oscoda's* mission, it was risky. "The fewer people who know about what's onboard the *Oscoda,* the better."

"Whiteford, what am I sending my people into?" Reed asked.

Tasia sighed, "What has been a trap from the beginning, I fear." She watched as *Feather's Edge* gently settled onto the apron. "There are only two diplomats onboard the *Oscoda.*"

Reed crossed his arms. "We were to retrieve seven."

Tasia nodded, "The others are prisoners of war. They were the leverage used to arrange the peace treaty. It seems as though the Eastern Coalition had no interest in peace after all, just getting their people back."

Reed pinched the bridge of his nose. "So it's not some small, rough nation we are going up against."

"No," Tasia stated, "It's the whole fucking Coalition military."

Reed shook his head, "One ship against an entire air force. I see your concern."

Tasia sighed, mulling over her next statement, "I do question why you cleared the *Stanton* for active service. I originally assigned *Express* for a reason."

Tasia saw Reed look away, "I was told it was for ceremonial purposes. I figured the *Juliane* and *Lancer* would have been doing most of the work."

Tasia nodded and looked back at *Feather's Edge*. Reed's answer had confirmed her fears. The change in ship assignment had been a request from the diplomats on *Oscoda,* backed by its Captain. She turned away from the airfield. It could only mean one thing: the *Oscoda* was compromised.

"This is your mess, Reed," Tasia stated bluntly. "I'd hate to see the repercussions if you fail to bring the *Stanton* and her crew home."

Patrick Gloutney

WCN *Stanton*

Vincent walked along the damaged generator with Harris at his side. "Anything new?"

Harris shook his head, "I inspected the fire and safety systems. Everything seems fine now."

"That's positive," Vincent remarked. "This is going to take some work."

"You ever had to make this kind of repair before?" Harris asked.

"Once," Vincent remarked. "When we were testing that weapon the first time, it blew out both generators."

Harris chuckled, shaking his head, "I'm sure that was an electrifying experience."

Vincent turned to Harris, a small smile on his face, "That was terrible."

Harris lightly punched Vincent on the shoulder, "Got you to smile though."

Vincent nodded and turned back to his inspection. He was glad to have Harris. The engineer's eagerness to keep morale up made up for Vincent's somewhat cynical nature.

"How many more punches do you think she can take?" Harris asked.

Vincent shrugged, "Honestly, we are running on borrowed time. Speaking of, has anyone checked the hull patches?"

Harris nodded, "Some are leaking. Repair crews are working on it. I have regular hull inspections being done as well."

"Good thinking." Vincent pulled open a panel on the Generator Control Unit, or GCU. "We should check the bilge system too. Make sure it can still keep—" Vincent stopped as he examined the Generator Control Unit. "What the hell?"

"What did you find?" Harris inquired, moving closer.

"I don't know," Vincent responded, examining the GCU. closer, "Does that look right to you?"

Harris leaned in and shook his head, "It's not wired like any GCU. I've seen."

Vincent nodded, "If this was wired wrong, it could explain why it didn't stop the generator from overloading."

"Right, but why would it be wired like that in the first place?"

Vincent thought back on his inspections when they were decommissioning the ship, "It was wired properly when we left port. I reinstalled this unit myself."

Harris took a step back, resting his hands on his head, "Does that mean what I think it means?"

"Check the other GCU," Vincent answered. "Then we'll see."

Feather's Edge

Tyler let out an exasperated sigh as he flipped through the papers in front of him. *It's too rushed,* he thought to himself, looking over a hydraulic schematic for the rear cargo door on the aircraft. He had barely had time to study *Feather's Edge* before they had been deployed, and there was no way he could learn everything in time. His addition, the crew had proven effective in allowing *Feather's Edge* to defend itself, but he worried about his ability to be helpful if systems started failing. A bump from turbulence made his binder fall off his lap and onto the floor of the cargo bay. Tyler let out a groan and watched out the window as the sun set on the horizon on the horizon over the sea. They must have been closing in on the first carrier. The *Phantoms* likely already reached it by now.

Tyler picked up his things before walking to the rear cargo door. In the last practice run, he hadn't even opened the door. He examined the controls, and they looked straightforward enough, but he didn't know what the door's limitations were. He shook his head; the situation where they were going must be dire if they were taking this much risk with a multi-million-dollar prototype aircraft.

"Strafer!" Flint called from the forward bulkhead, "Catch!" She threw a water bottle at him.

"Thanks," Tyler answered before setting it down with the rest of his stuff.

"Enjoying the flight, lover boy?" Flint asked.

"It's fine," Tyler stated, looking at the rather uncomfortable canvas seats lining the wall, "The inflight service kind of sucks though."

Flint let out a laugh, "You're quick. I like that."

Tyler flinched, his mind flashing back to his inability to save his fighter, "Not quick enough."

Flint nodded, "We've started our descent towards the carrier. Feather wants to run a loading practice run so I can show you the cargo ramp."

"Good idea," Tyler remarked.

Flint was silent for a moment before she walked up to Strafer, "Get your head out of that plane. It's buried in the sand. You are here now."

"How did you—"

"You think you're the first pilot I've seen screw up?" Flint asked.

Tyler flinched again. "You think so too?"

Flint shrugged, "I could lie and say no, but knowing the problem that fighter had, I wouldn't have risked the trailing position you were in."

Tyler shook his head with a sigh, further proof of his stupidity, "Great, thanks."

"Don't give me that," Flint snapped, "You think you are the only dumb ass that crashed an airplane? We're test pilots. Comes with the territory."

"Doesn't mean—"

Flint rolled her eyes. "Shut it. I've damaged aircraft, Sam smashed the gear off an aircraft she was flying. Even Claire landed this rig wrong and totalled an engine. We all make mistakes, Tyler. The difference between a bad pilot and a good one is what we do about it."

Tyler was silent for a moment, surprised at the rather in-tune statement from the usually brash W.S.O. before he nodded, "You're right."

A tone sounded through the cargo bay, "That's the warning, put on your mask and I'll show you the ropes."

Tyler nodded and got his gear on, "Thanks, Flint."

Flint smiled, "Anytime."

"Com check," Feather's voice called over the intercom. Both Tyler and Flint answered. Before long, they were hovering, and Feather called for the ramp to be lowered. Flint walked Tyler through getting it down. He was surprised at just how turbulent the airflow around the gate was when the aircraft was hovering.

"We can't get all the way down to the deck, so they have to climb this rope ladder the rest of the way," Flint explained, "That means you have to be at the end of the ramp helping."

"And if you guys move suddenly?" Tyler asked, noticing how little there would be to hold onto during that part of the mission.

Flint smirked, "Grab onto something. And whatever you do, don't fall into the water."

Patrick Gloutney

WCN *Stanton*

"Sabotage?" Delmar asked in disbelief. "Are you sure?"

Vincent nodded, "We found at least three other systems that had been tampered with. Each failure could be mistaken for the ship simply showing its age."

"So, all the trouble we've been having has been deliberate?" Delmar asked.

Vincent shifted uncomfortably on his feet, "Not quite, Sir. The ship is still very much showing its age. This is the first instance of sabotage we've had."

"Why the generators?" LeCroix asked.

Vincent shrugged, "Depends on how much they know about the ship. Whether intended or not, that generator could have blown during battle when I fired a weapon."

Delmar shook his head, "Robbing us of not only power and propulsion in likely the most critical time, but also pulling you away from the weapons controls. Let's assume that was the saboteur's intent. Who could have done this?"

Vincent nodded and flipped through his notes, "Any of the engineering staff."

"Any of them?" LeCroix asked, an edge in his voice. "Even you?"

Vincent raised an eyebrow, "I don't need to sabotage the ship like this to destroy it."

"What the hell does that mean?" LeCroix demanded.

"You are dismissed, LeCroix," Delmar stated sternly.

"Sir, I—"

"Are being unprofessional. You are dismissed. You can report back to me when you are ready to start acting like an Executive Officer. Am I clear?"

"Crystal, Sir," LeCroix snapped before he left. Vincent let himself relax for the first time since walking into the room.

Delmar sighed and shook his head, "Forgive him, Mr. Travis. This is just adding to an already stressful command."

"Understandable, Sir," Vincent answered. "Perhaps my response was out of place."

Delmar chuckled, "What are we going to do about this sabotage, Mr. Travis?"

"I intend on limiting access to ship vitals to only those I trust, if you'll allow me."

Delmar nodded, "As long as you aren't overworking your crewmen, I am fine with it."

"I'll get you a list of those that worry me," Vincent stated before he turned to leave.

"You need not fear me, Mr. Travis," Delmar called suddenly, causing Vincent to freeze in his tracks.

"Pardon, Sir?"

"You don't have to consider me a friend," Delmar began, "But I am not like your other Captains. You will not be at fault for anything that has occurred on this ship."

Vincent grimaced, memories of past arguments, disagreements, reprimands, and beatings flashing through his eyes, "I don't know what you're talking about, Sir."

Delmar nodded with a sigh, "That's fine. Just know I read your file, all of it. I'm on your side."

"I appreciate that, Sir," Vincent answered, his voice tense but hope burning in his chest. He hoped he could, just maybe, trust Captain Delmar.

Delmar stood and walked to the door, opening it for Vincent, "And if anything makes you fear for your safety or that of this ship, bring it to my attention, please. Anything, or anyone."

Vincent eyed the captain momentarily before nodding and stepping out into the hallway. He paused and turned back to the captain, "Sir?"

"He will be dealt with, Mr. Travis," Delmar stated, "I promise you that."

Patrick Gloutney

WCN Aircraft Carrier Hasta

"Seriously?" Sam asked in shock.

"Yeah," Flint answered as they walked through the halls of the Aircraft Carrier *Hasta* towards the flight deck. "Is it so hard to believe?"

Sam stopped and raised an eyebrow, "Kind of yeah. How old were you?"

"Older than you'd believe," Flint shot back, "Parents were big into it. Took me a while to realize it wasn't for me."

Sam shook her head and started walking again, "Ok. But like you did contemporary stuff, right?"

Flint chuckled, "What, you don't appreciate the classics?"

Sam laughed, "I just can't see you ever wearing pink."

Flint gasped, "So quick to judge. I'll have you know I was fetching in pink."

Sam climbed the stairs to a higher deck. "Please tell me you are messing with me."

"I wish," Flint answered, following quickly up the stairs. "Wasted years studying ballet."

"And you decide to bring this up, why?" Sam asked, turning back to face the W.S.O.

Flint smiled, "To give you a break. We've all been wound so tight by this mission; we need to talk about something else for a change."

Sam clucked her tongue, "You're noticing it too?"

Flint nodded, "Hard not to. You're doing a good job with Feather. But I was worried about you. Well, you and Strafer."

"Strafer?" Sam asked. She had been so focused on making sure Feather was handling everything well, she hadn't even thought about his coping since they left.

Flint nodded, "He's wound tighter than anyone. He's trying to learn *Feather's Edge* inside and out when all he has to do is push a button to lower the ramp."

Sam stepped over a bulkhead. "Why? He's fine based on the last test runs."

Flint shrugged, "Losing that Phantom Jet in the desert got to him, it seems. If I had to guess, he feels betrayed by his aircraft. Doesn't help that his girl-friend may as well be an aircraft."

Sam stopped. "Greaser?"

"I forget how insightful you can be," Sam muttered.

Flint winked, "In more ways than one, girl."

Sam rolled her eyes. "You think Strafer's worried Feather's going to betray him?"

Flint shrugged again, "Not that far of a stretch. Especially with how order-bound she is. I can't imagine how hard it is for him to grasp their reality."

Sam sighed and stepped out onto the flight deck, only for Telos to brush past her rudely and rush down the hallway they had come from.

"Speaking of someone who needs to re—" Sam began, only to stop when she saw *Feather's Edge*.

"Shit," Flint swore. *Feather's Edge*, for lack of a better description, looked defeated. It sat low on its suspension, its flaps extended and cannons facing the ground. Its windows were tinted black so you couldn't see inside, and even its rotors seemed to droop more than usual, though it was likely an illusion. Not many in the program wanted to acknowledge it, but the link between *Feather's Edge* and Feather was a two-way street, and if what they were seeing was any indication, Feather was not in a good mood. It looked to be the worst display of depression she had ever seen on the aircraft.

Now that's an odd thought, Sam thought bitterly. "I need to find Feather."

"Damn I never thought an aircraft could look that sad," Flint remarked, "I hope nothing's damaged."

Sam nodded, even though it was part of her job to deal with these sorts of things it never ceased to shake her to see just how badly Feather could be hurting.

"You've got to fix her, Sam," Flint remarked, "Because if she flies like that thing looks...we are all dead."

Patrick Gloutney

WCN *Stanton*

Delmar rubbed the bridge of his nose as he pored over the most recent naval intelligence report they had received. They may have had a reprieve from attacks since the storm, but they were going to pay for it. The latest intelligence showed a large naval battle group making its way toward the *Stanton* and the *Oscoda*. They had made an impression, and the Eastern Coalition wasn't holding anything back on their next attempt. Estimates put the Coalition battle group's arrival before any of the Western Council ships would reach them.

Repairs were underway on the damaged generator from the storm, but with inspection revealing more and more sabotaged systems, it was unclear what would last in a battle. Even with full armament Delmar was unsure they could stand their ground against this entire battle group, let alone crippled like they were now. Delmar hoped that perhaps their ships could get within range of air cover to get the diplomats out of harm's way. Then they could run.

He wasn't even sure if they could outrun them. The Coalition battle group's estimated top speed was the same as the *Stanton* according to Travis, but that was only if they could keep both engines running near full power. Travis had cautioned against pushing the engines that hard for an extended period unless left with no choice.

A knock on the door pulled Delmar from his thoughts. "Enter."

"You asked to see me, Sir?" LeCroix stated as he entered.

Delmar nodded, "Have you seen the latest intel report?"

"Yes, Sir. Looks grim."

Delmar sighed. He twirled a pen between his fingers before leaning back in his chair, "Yes, it is. I want you to answer my next question carefully."

"Sir?" LeCroix asked, tilting his head to the side.

"I'm going to give you one chance to tell me what happened when you brought the *Lancer* crew to see Travis."

LeCroix's eyes shifted with obvious unease, "I don't—"

"I said, think carefully, LeCroix," Delmar interjected.

LeCroix was silent for a moment before speaking, "The *Lancer* crew expressed their displeasure physically."

Delmar nodded, "And you let it happen?"

LeCroix met Delmar's gaze, "You've seen his file. Filled with counts of misconduct and insubordination."

Delmar leaned forward in his chair, "Why lie about it? Why call it an accident?"

LeCroix was silent. Delmar sighed, "Because you knew I wouldn't approve."

"I felt it was not worth your time, given the situation."

Delmar shook his head and stood up, "The well-being of my crew is worth every second, LeCroix. A philosophy you should consider adopting."

"Travis is a detriment to our crew. His disciplinary file proves that! We don't need him."

"Follow me," Delmar commanded. They made their way through the halls until they reached the upper decks. Once above decks, he pointed to the blue fins on the ship's superstructure. "Tell me what those are and what they do."

LeCroix faltered, "They...They're one of our weapons."

Delmar nodded, "That is why we need Mr. Travis. You and I have seen the same report on these weapons, yet neither of us knows anything about them."

"We could easily learn, Sir," LeCroix protested, "Or task Harris."

"And then make a misstep and destroy the whole ship," Delmar finished, "I want you to stay away from Mr. Travis. Like it or not, we need him."

"Captain—"

"And let me be perfectly clear; any form of harassment, physical or mental, will not be allowed on board my ship," Delmar stated sternly. "Understood?"

"Yes, Captain."

Delmar shook his head, "From this point forward, Travis's word is to be treated as if it were my own. What would you call it if you treated me the way you treated Mr. Travis yesterday?"

LeCroix swallowed, "Insubordination. Sir."

Delmar nodded, locking eyes with LeCroix, "And what would that call for?"

LeCroix looked away, "Immediate dismissal from Command."

Patrick Gloutney

WCN Hasta

Sam cursed under her breath when *Feather's Edge* refused to open its door to her. Her search for *Feather* had quickly turned up nothing. She was hoping that if *Feather* was having an episode, she might go to the one familiar thing onboard, *Feather's Edge*. Unfortunately for Sam, it was locked up tight, and there was no way for her to get in. A design flaw, if there ever was one, in Sam's opinion, but the issue had never been addressed.

Sam banged on the metal skin of the aircraft, "Feather open up." There was no response. Sam shook her head, "C'mon, Feather, it's me. Talk to me."

Sam tried the door again, only for it to open. She let out a sigh of relief, stepping inside the aircraft and closing the door behind her. As she expected, the aircraft was dark inside. *If I had only known what I was signing up for*, Sam thought as her eyes fell on Feather, her legs pulled tight against her chest, head down. *Poor girl is tormented by her so-called enhancements.* Sam took a seat next to Feather and leaned against the cool metal wall.

"So," Sam began after a moment of silence, "Nice weather we're having." Sam smiled when she heard Feather chuckle, though it was still laced with sorrow. They sat in silence for a few more moments till Sam rolled her neck, "You want to talk about it?" Feather shook her head. "Then why did you let me in?"

Feather took an unsteady breath, "I screwed up."

Sam cocked her head to the side, "How?"

Feather banged the back of her head against the wall, "Following stupid orders."

"You've lost me," Sam remarked, resting a hand on Feather's shoulder. "What orders?"

Feather shook her head, eyes screwed shut, "I was ordered to cut ties with Tyler. Reed and Boudreaux felt it was a conflict of interest."

Of course, they did, Sam thought. Not that they were wrong. "I take it you carried them out already."

Feather nodded, "I'm such an idiot."

Sam sighed, "Feather, it's okay. I'm sure Strafer will understand."

"And next time?" Feather snapped, "Or the time after that? How is he supposed to love someone who will turn on him with just an order? He wants commitment, not this. I'm so screwed up they could order me to kill him and I would have no choice."

Sam grimaced; from what she knew of Feather's condition, she wasn't wrong. "How did Strafer take it?"

Feather winced, "Not well. It hurt him so much."

"Do you want me to try and explain the situation to him?"

Feather shook her head, "No, he deserves better. I won't put him through that again."

"Claire..." Sam began, but then paused, "What can I do?"

Feather was quiet for a while before she spoke, "Can you bring me back in time before this project starts? Before I volunteer to be a stupid test pilot for this stupid aircraft."

Sam shook her head, "Believe me, I would if I could Claire. You don't deserve this." A heavy silence fell on the cargo bay once again, "You going to be okay to fly?"

Feather nodded, "I've been ordered to be. I have no choice."

WCN Hasta

"That's a lot of firepower," Flint remarked, rubbing her temple. Reed had just finished briefing them on the Eastern Coalition's battle group heading for the *Stanton*. "A carrier and everything."

Reed nodded, "More than even our best estimates." A tense silence filled the small room. Tyler shook his head, eyes drifting to the worried faces of each aviator in the meeting. He locked eyes with Feather before quickly looking away, a fresh wave of heartache racing through him. He shook his head again to clear his mind. He knew he had to stay focused, but that task wasn't proving easy.

"At top speed, our ships won't be within range to provide weapons cover before the Eastern Coalition vessels are within firing range. However, Intelligence suggests that we have a greater air cover range," Reed sighed.

"Meaning we could get in and out before they can launch fighters?" Greaser asked.

"We are too far away for that." Reed handed her a report, "This is our best guess as to what you'll encounter."

Greaser laughed and passed the report to Feather, who didn't even look at the report, her eyes still on Tyler. "Great, we both arrive at the same time."

"That's pushing our fuel range too," Flint remarked, after snatching the report from Feather.

"Same with us," Gypsy stated.

"I'm not asking for problems," Reed stated, "I want solutions. This is our best chance before we have to face both air and sea-based attacks on the *Oscoda*."

"He's got a point," Tyler remarked, "The longer we delay, the worse it becomes."

Reed nodded, "I want you all launching at the earliest opportunity. Is that clear?"

"Yes, Sir," the room answered.

"Good. Dismissed," Reed commanded, taking his leave. A crushing silence followed. Tyler shook his head and stood to leave. He got to the hall before a call stopped him.

"Tyler?" Feather's voice called. Tyler wanted to ignore her, to keep walking and pretend he hadn't heard her, but he couldn't force himself to. He turned to see Feather closing the door to the briefing room. She looked so small.

"What?" Tyler asked, his voice cold.

Feather flinched. She rubbed her neck and sighed, "I'm so sorry."

This time, Tyler flinched. He hadn't even realized how much he loved her until she had shattered his heart. It felt like a lead weight was in his gut, and reminding him of everything only served to further his pain.

"You should be," Tyler stated simply and turned to leave.

"I'd change my orders if I could," Feather called again.

Tyler snarled, "Because that's all that matters, isn't it?"

"It's not that simple," Feather stressed.

Tyler turned on her, "Tell me Feather, aren't your aircraft limitations in a way orders?"

Feather shrank back, "That's different—"

"Unbelievable. You'd disobey orders for your plane but not for me," Tyler stated harshly.

Feather straightened, "At least I can comply with my maintenance restrictions."

Tyler flinched, his shoulders sagging. She thought he was a fool, just like the rest. It was little wonder that she jumped at the chance to end things.

Feather seemed to realize what she had said as she quickly covered her mouth, "Tyler, I'm so sorry. I didn't—"

"If that is all. Good day, Lieutenant," Tyler stated sharply, leaving before Feather could respond.

Patrick Gloutney

Feather's Edge

"All systems green," Sam called as they sped towards the *Stanton* and the *Oscoda*.

"Phantoms check in," Feather ordered.

"One," Telos called.

"Two," Gypsy responded before both Phantom jets took position on either side of *Feather's Edge*.

"Phantoms in position," Telos reported.

"Confirmed," Sam answered.

"Confirmed," Feather called. Sam kept an eye on Feather. She seemed fine, but deep down she knew the pilot wasn't.

"Strafer, you ready?" Sam called back through the intercom.

"Yes, Ma'am," Strafer's response came. Strafer had been less effective at hiding his emotions than Feather. Sam could tell that Feather's cold and professional persona wasn't making anything easier on him. She could only hope it didn't impede his abilities.

"Damn, girls we've got a problem," Flint called, "Twelve...no...sixteen airborne contacts heading for the *Oscoda*."

"Confirm sixteen?" Telos asked.

"Negative now eighteen," Flint responded.

Sam shook her head, "I hope that EMP is working."

"Of yah," Flint said sarcastically, "The one thing we haven't tested our defences against."

"Should be fine..." Feather stated, "In theory. When will the contacts reach the *Oscoda*."

"Estimate two minutes after us at present speed," Flint answered.

Sam quickly ran a calculation on her kneeboard, "We have the fuel to increase speed."

Feather nodded; they were just a few minutes out from the two ships. "Phantoms break early. Do what you can to keep them busy."

"Phantom one," Telos acknowledged as the two fighter jets pulled ahead of *Feather's Edge*.

"Ready for this?" Feather asked.

Sam nodded, "You've got this." Feather pushed *Feather's Edge* lower to the water. Soon enough, they could see the two ships they were aiming for. The *Stanton* looked to be maneuvering to a defensive position around the *Oscoda*. They sped over the *Stanton* banking to show off their colour so they wouldn't be mistaken as hostile before turning to the *Oscoda*.

"Stable," Feather called after she maneuvered *Feather's Edge* into position over the *Oscoda*.

"Loading underway," Strafer called.

Sam nodded and started the timer, "Five minutes."

"Contact's bearing three-five-zero one minute out," Flint reported.

"Can you lock them?" Feather asked Sam.

"Weapons locked," Flint answered, "And away." Two missiles sped forward, pulling a turn towards their targets.

"Two confirmed hits," Flint reported. "Contact's scattering and regrouping. Phantoms are breaking the group up."

No one spoke as they waited for Flint's next report. Sam could tell Feather was having trouble holding the aircraft steady in the gusty winds.

"Two minutes," she called, "You alright, Feather?"

"Fine," Feather muttered, "Remind me why there's no helipad?"

"They were on a budget?" Flint offered. An uneasy chuckle came from Feather.

"Fuck," Flint swore, "Contacts at bearings three-four-zero, zero-five-zero, one-six-zero, two-seven-zero. All equal distance."

Surrounding us, "I can't fire on all of them at once."

"Strafer halt loading, raise the ramp," Feather ordered.

"I've only got two more," Strafer countered.

"Targets closing fast," Flint called.

"That's an order, Strafer," Feather snapped, "Flint, on my mark, raise the ramp."

Sam glanced at Feather; they both knew what she was risking if they moved without confirmation that Strafer was inside the cargo bay.

"Ramp is still down," Sam cautioned.

"Four missile locks!" Flint called as the warning tone sounded.

"Tyler, ass inside now," Feather yelled, "Flint ramp up."

"Ramps coming up," Flint responded.

"Countermeasures. Engines zero," Feather called out as she moved. *Feather's Edge* leaped forward past the edge of the *Oscoda's* deck.

"That's low Feather!" Sam cautioned as they fell towards the sea before levelling just above the waves and speeding away. The missile lock tone silenced as they rocketed forward.

"Contact bearing three-six-zero," Flint cautioned, "Angle's wrong for weapons."

"Check that," Feather said. Sam watched as the enemy fighter flew right over them. "Engine one 45 degrees." Before Sam could question it, *Feather's*

Edge pulled into a skidding left-hand climbing turn. Alarms blared in the cockpit as the engines were never meant to be set at two different angles.

"Lock and Fire," Feather ordered as they came up behind the enemy fighter. "Engines both zero." The fighter erupted into flames ahead of them, *Feather's Edge* being rocked by the turbulence caused by the explosion. Sam let out a sigh of relief, but it was short-lived.

"Contacts now bearing one-six-zero moving one-eight-zero and zero-one-zero moving three-six-zero."

"Driving us into a game of chicken," Sam said as she saw Feather readjust her grip on the throttles.

"Call time to impact," Feather ordered.

"Twenty seconds," Flint responded.

Sam queued the intercom, "Strafer, if anyone isn't strapped down, buckle up." There was no response.

"Ten seconds," Flint called, "Nine, eight, seven, six,"

"Engine's 90 degrees," Feather called, forcing *Feather's Edge* into a steep climb. They could hear the two enemy fighters collide behind them.

"Pitch fifteen degrees, engine 45 degrees," Feather called as she established a rapid ascent. In no time at all, they were passing ten thousand feet.

Sam scanned her instruments before something caught her eye, "Phantom nine o'clock!" she yelled. She heard the engines roll back and felt *Feather's Edge* come to almost a dead stop in the air seconds before one of the Phantoms flew past her nose. Then *Feather's Edge* began falling backward. Sam tensed; they had never done this kind of maneuver before, and their engines didn't like reverse airflow.

A warning tone and light confirmed her fears as *Feather's Edge* began to tip over into a spin, "Flameout engine one!"

WCN *Stanton*

"Warning: weapons failure," the computer called seconds after the Electro-Magnetic Pulse generator was supposed to be fired.

Delmar let out a frustrated groan. "Shields up." The plan had been to wipe out the enemy forces with an EMP once they got close enough so that the rescue party wouldn't have to deal with them. But after three failed attempts at firing the weapon, it looked like they weren't getting that help.

"Missile!" Someone called just before it hit the shields, lurching the *Stanton* to the side.

"We need that EMP, Mr. Travis," Delmar called on the intercom.

"Working on it," Travis's response came.

Delmar drummed his fingers on the console in front of him as he watched the battle unfold. He eyed the rescue aircraft, *Feather's Edge,* in a hover that must have been just feet off the deck of the *Oscoda.* It was a testament to the pilot's skill, especially considering the gusty winds outside. If the reports he was hearing were any indication, the help they had been sent was greatly outnumbered. He watched as reports of aircraft converging on the *Oscoda* flowed through the bridge.

"Travis, ready the secondary plasma weapons array," Delmar ordered. His studying of the ship's weapons had certainly helped him develop a better strategy for this battle. But he shared Travis's concerns about overusing them, especially the primary plasma weapons.

"Weapons ready," Travis called back.

"Shields down. Fire." Delmar ordered. The shields disappeared around *Stanton*. Delmar watched as light from flares and chaff erupted from the rescue aircraft's tail before it lunged forward, dipping low towards the sea to avoid the oncoming attack.

"Targets acquired," the computer called just before it fired. Four beams of orange light erupted from small plasma cannons situated around the ship. They fired for just under a second before the computer called: "Two targets destroyed."

"Shields up. Come around heading zero-niner-zero," Delmar ordered to bring the ship closer to the *Oscoda*. An aircraft flew towards them, machine guns raking their shields. The Coalition pilot, unaware of what he was doing, adjusted his course to pass just overhead the *Stanton* and flew right into her shields, erupting into flames.

The two *Phantom* jets screamed overhead, scattering another formation of Coalition fighters.

"Missile contact bearing two-seven-zero," the radar operator reported. Delmar turned his gaze in that direction to see the missile heading toward the *Phantoms*.

"Can we lock on to it?" Delmar asked.

"Negative, Sir."

Delmar cursed as the *Phantoms* broke formation to evade.

"Targets acquired," the computer called, having locked the plasma weapons on other fighters.

"Shields down. Fire," Delmar ordered. The shields fell, and the weapons fired. The enemy took advantage of this; however, one fighter dove on the *Stanton* from above, raking it with gunfire.

"Targets destroyed," the computer called.

"Shields up," Delmar commanded. The shield raised, but not before the enemy fighter had managed to damage one of the secondary plasma weapons.

"EMP ready," Travis called over the intercom.

"Are you sure?" Delmar asked as another group of fighters made a pass, the shields protecting the ship.

There was a long pause, "As sure as anything onboard."

"Prepare it to fire."

"Warning EMP discharge in ten, nine, eight," the computer called.

"Shields down," Delmar ordered. Truth be told, he wasn't clear if the shields interfered with the EMP generator, but he figured better safe than sorry. He watched as *Feather's Edge* shot into a near-vertical climb before two aircraft collided head-on behind them.

Hell of a pilot, Delmar thought. Then a *Phantom* jet sped overhead a missile on its tail. That pilot wasn't fast enough, just before the EMP was about to discharge, another missile decimated the fighter jet.

All the displays on the bridge went dark for a split second before coming back to life. "EMP Discharged," the computer called. Delmar let out the breath he was holding and looked around to see if the EMP had worked. Every remaining fighter was falling from the sky, along with *Feather's Edge*.

Patrick Gloutney

Feather's Edge

"I need hydraulics!" Feather called. Alarms blared as *Feather's Edge* spun towards the sea. With the loss of their number one engine, they had been sent into a spin where they were essentially rotating around a non-flying wing. They had recovered from them before, but something was off this time.

"Sam, help," Feather ordered. Sam quickly complied and pressed as hard as she could on the rudder. Feather was right, though; there wasn't much hydraulic pressure. She glanced at the hydraulic pressure gauges.

"Hyd System one and two are gone," she called.

"Five thousand," Flint called, reminding her crewmates of their rapidly depleting altitude.

"Deploy the RAT," Feather ordered. The RAT, or Ram Air Turbine, was designed to supply basic hydraulic and electrical systems and was meant for a two-engine out situation. Sam didn't question the order. Eventually, between Sam and Feather, they were able to get enough rudder authority to stop the spin and pull out of the dive just a thousand feet above the water.

Feather let out a heavy sigh. "Number One Engine Air Start Checklist." They went through the checklist and, before long, had both engines running again.

"Hydraulics normal," Sam called.

"Contacts?" Feather requested.

Flint was silent for a moment, "Damn, it must have worked."

"What worked?" Sam asked.

"The EMP No airborne enemy contacts," Flint reported, though there seemed to be a puzzled tone to her voice.

"Strafer, how many passengers did we get?" Feather asked.

That couldn't have been fun in the back, Sam thought to herself as no answer came.

"Strafer report," Feather tried again before shaking her head. "Flint?"

"On it," Flint answered, unbuckling.

"How's our fuel?" Feather asked.

Sam quickly ran the numbers, "Low, we may have to come back another time for the rest."

"Damn," Feather muttered.

Sam nodded, "Good flying, Feather."

There was no response from Feather till Flint came back, "Well?"

"We got them all," Flint answered, her voice hollow.

"And Tyler?" Feather pushed.

Flint seemed to hesitate, causing Sam to look back at their W.S.O., "He's not back there. He must have fallen out."

Sam's eyes widened as she saw Feather's knuckles go white from gripping the controls too tightly. She also noticed a fluctuation in the number two engine's rpm. "Easy Feather."

"He's gone?" Feather asked.

"It wasn't that far a fall," Flint reasoned, "the *Oscoda* crew will pick him up."

"We're going back," Feather announced.

"We don't have the fuel," Sam argued.

She could almost see the internal battle raging in Feather, the need to try and keep both *Feather's Edge* and Strafer safe pitted one against the other. "Fucking damn it all to hell." Sam flinched, not used to hearing Feather speak that way. "Phantoms report!"

"Phantom one, climbing through fifteen thousand, at bingo fuel on the way home."

"Phantom two?" Feather asked after a long moment of silence.

"Phantom two was lost," Telos's voice answered, "No chutes as far as I can tell."

Feather shook her head, "*Feather's Edge* is free and clear with a full payload. Good work, Telos." With that, Feather adjusted their course and made for the carrier.

Sam barely caught Feather muttering, "Please be right, Flint. Please be right," to herself as she set up for maximum range flight.

WCN *Stanton,*

Delmar couldn't believe his eyes as aircraft rained down from the sky. One struck the *Stantons'* shields before falling into the sea. It looked like a scene from an aviator's worst nightmare. *And it's not even our most lethal weapon.*

Delmar's eyes turned to watch as *Feather's Edge* just barely managed to recover from its dive. He prayed their troubles were unrelated. He shook his head; it reinforced his worries over the EMP generator. "Systems check?"

"All major systems are reporting operational. Travis is reporting there is a strain on the number one electrical system," LeCroix answered.

Delmar nodded, "Maintain a defensive position with the *Oscoda.* What's the status of that battle group?"

"Turning away," the report came back. Delmar let out a sigh of relief. He wasn't sure the *Stanton* could survive an attack from an entire naval battle group.

"*Feather's Edge* reported mission success," LeCroix spoke up. "All diplomats accounted for."

Applause and cheers erupted on the bridge as Delmar smiled. It was over, they could finally go home.

"Shields down," Delmar ordered, "Let's pick up the *Oscoda* crew and get underway before they regroup."

LeCroix nodded, and Delmar turned back to look out at the *Oscoda*. That's when he noticed something odd. The water behind its stern was churning. The *Oscoda* was moving under its power.

That shouldn't be possible, Delmar pondered. "LeCroix?"

"Sir?" LeCroix asked, coming over as he was called.

"Am I seeing things?" Delmar asked.

LeCroix peered out the window just as the *Oscoda* turned towards the *Stanton*. "What the hell?" LeCroix muttered.

Delmar was about to call for Travis when he noticed the shape of the *Oscoda* flicker. His eyes widened when he realized what that might mean. The *Oscoda* flickered again before the hologram around the ship disappeared, revealing a Coalition Warship with its weapons trained on the *Stanton*.

"Shields Up!" It was too late; the Coalition ship fired before the shields activated.

WCN *Stanton*

"All ahead full, come heading zero-five-zero!" Delmar ordered. "Weapons to bearing zero-nine-zero." He steadied himself as another shot from the Coalition warship pelted their shields. The first shot had severely damaged their rear turret, and Delmar watched as the only remaining turret swung to face the enemy.

"Travis, weapons status," he demanded.

"Primary weapons computer is offline," Travis reported, "Only conventional weapons are functional."

Another shot rocked the *Stanton's* shields, "Get me those weapons, Mr. Travis."

"The Coalition Naval fleet is turning our way," LeCroix reported.

Fell for a damn trap, Delmar berated himself. They needed to run, but if this was the Coalition Ship that he suspected it to be, it would easily outrun them. Another impact on the shields rocked the ship. He had no choice: "Shields down, return fire." The *Stanton's* remaining turret fired, its shot striking the deck of the Coalition ship. "Shields up," Delmar ordered to block another incoming enemy shell just in time. The way the enemy ship was firing on them worried him. It wasn't shooting to kill; they were trying to maim. The shots seemed to fall with precision, right where the remaining weapons would have been. It brought a sinking realization to Delmar. The diplomats on the *Oscoda* had never been the target. It had been the *Stanton* all along.

"Turret three has jammed Sir," LeCroix reported.

Delmar slammed his fist into the console in front of him as the Coalition warship began a barrage of weapons fire on the *Stanton's* shields. "Travis, give me something before those shields give out."

"Working on it," Travis' reply came. "Turn your head onto them."

"Turning head one-five-zero," Delmar ordered. The *Stanton* crashed through the surf as it swung to face the Coalition warship. The enemy likewise turned their way, still pelting the ship with weapon fire.

"Sir, you can't ram it!" LeCroix protested.

Delmar clenched his fists praying Travis knew what he was doing, "Got a better idea, LeCroix?"

No response came as the computer announced, "Target acquired. Course locked."

"Hard left rudder!" LeCroix ordered.

"Belay that order," Delmar countered, intent on letting Travis's plan play out.

"Ship's not responding to the control inputs!" Helm reported.

The collision alarm sounded through the bridge, "Brace, Brace, Brace," the computer called.

"All stop!" LeCroix desperately called.

"Belay that order! LeCroix, you are relieved from duty," Delmar ordered seconds before the two ships collided.

WCN Oscoda's – Last Known Position

Tyler stared in disbelief from afar, bobbing in the water. The shot from what had been the *Oscoda* decimated the rear turret on the *Stanton*. The *Stanton* was quick to react; its remaining turret swung towards the *Oscoda* imposter while a second shot exploded on the *Stanton's* shields. Tyler had never before felt so helpless, drifting on the surface as these two ships locked horns. He resisted the urge to activate his emergency locator for fear that it would attract the wrong attention at this moment.

It seemed that despite taking the *Stanton* by surprise, the Coalition Warship still moved with caution. It's as though it was testing the *Stantons'* defences while the two ships circled each other. A shot from the *Stanton* erupted on the deck of the Coalition Warship. The shot was answered, but the *Stantons'* shields were up in time. The Coalition Warship started a barrage of shots peppering the shields of the *Stanton* in response. The weapons fire was so loud it began to hurt Tyler's ears even from his distance.

C'mon, Stanton, Tyler urged as he watched the *Stanton* try and maneuver away from the Coalition Warship. It seemed that was what the Coalition ship was waiting for, however. A missile rocketed off its deck towards the *Stanton,* adding to the barrage of weapons fire. The Coalition certainly wasn't holding anything back. That's when the *Stanton* did something Tyler wasn't expecting. It turned head-on into the weapons fire. The Coalition warship responded by turning to meet the *Stanton*, the two ships steaming head-on at one another. More weapons fire erupted, blasting the *Stanton's* shields once again as she crashed through the surf.

Tyler began to wonder just how long those shields could hold out as a beam of bright blue light extended from the *Stanton's* shields on either side. The two ships were closing at a frightening speed, with neither seeming willing to give up their game of chicken and give the other the advantage. Tyler could only watch as the two ships passed each other. He couldn't tell how close they were from his angle, but it looked like mere feet. He was expecting them to exchange more weapons fire, but there was no sound except the wind and the water lapping at his ears. The *Stanton* cleared the Coalition Warship's stern and began to circle, the beams of the light fading.

Tyler looked back at the enemy warship and noticed that it seemed to be slowing. *Holy shit,* Tyler thought as he realized what the *Stanton* had done. He watched in amazement as a series of shots from the *Stanton* caused the top half of the Coalition warship to slide clean off the rest of the hull into the water, causing what was left of the decapitated ship to capsize.

The *Stanton*, seemingly content with the damage it had done, stowed its weapons. Tyler couldn't tear his eyes away from the sinking Coalition Warship. One pass and the *Stanton* had sliced the ship in two. Fires began to erupt around the damaged vessel as sparks flew from the damaged systems. Tyler shuddered as the cries of men filled his ears. He quickly turned on his locator in hopes that the *Stanton* would retrieve him.

"Over here!" he yelled, waving his arms, though he knew it was useless at this distance. He could feel the cold of the water starting to seep into his bones. The *Stanton* sailed past the damaged warship before turning away and picking up speed.

"No! Don't! I'm over here!" Tyler yelled as his heart sank. It was running from the Coalition naval battle group, which meant he was left to fend for himself.

Patrick Gloutney

WCN *Stanton*

"You can't do this Captain!" LeCroix shouted as armed sailors moved to bring LeCroix to the brig.

"I was very clear in my stance on insubordination," Delmar stated. No one on the bridge dared speak.

"You were going to kill us all," LeCroix argued.

Delmar crossed his arms. "Are we dead, Mr. LeCroix?" Silence reigned, "I thought not." With that, LeCroix was dragged away. Delmar sighed and turned to look back at the capsized Coalition warship. He wasn't sure what weapon Travis had used, but it had been unsettlingly effective. Now running the engines at their maximum speed, Delmar only hoped they could return to their fleet before the Coalition battle group caught up with them.

Delmar grabbed the intercom, "Crew of the *Stanton,* this is your Captain speaking. I regret to inform you I have had to remove First Officer LeCroix from his Command on multiple counts of harassment of your fellow crewmembers and insubordination." Delmar paused. "This does not change anything on our mission. With our primary objective complete, we move to our most pressing matter: to survive."

Delmar looked to see all the bridge crew looking at him expectantly, "I won't sugar coat it. We have been set up and sabotaged on this entire mission. From crippled ship systems to a leaking hull, we have battled the odds and won. Now we are facing a Coalition battle group. They are likely newer, well-armed, and well-trained. but we are the *WCN Stanton*. This ship has fought and won battles alone before, and that will not change today. I need every man at their stations, every man's 100% as we demand 110% from our ship."

Delmar paused, taking a breath, "We are in retreat now and can match their speed, but it's unclear for how long. Know we don't do this for God or our country. We are fighting for our lives. To see our families and our loved ones back home again. If...no, when we lock horns with the Eastern Coalition ships, it will be them that quake in fear at the sound of our weapons fire. They will learn they have picked the wrong ship to try and take. They will fall. The *Stanton* will prevail." Delmar finished as applause erupted on the bridge.

"Sir! Emergency beacon in the water from *Feather's Edge.*"

"Position?" Delmar asked.

"Near the *Oscoda's* last position."

"Range to the Coalition battle group?"

"We are just outside weapons range, Sir."

Delmar scowled. It pained him to leave a man behind, but he needed every mile of space he could get between them and that battle group. Turning back now would mean putting the *Stanton* forever within range of enemy weapons, risking the lives of every crewman onboard.

"Status on the *Bandit*?" Delmar asked. The *Bandit* was a small, high-speed watercraft that they were carrying. It had been designed to catch up to large warships and plant explosives or drop boarding parties. Its speed meant it could potentially rescue the standard airman and still catch up to the *Stanton,* but it had been stored near the rear turret.

"It was destroyed in the conflict," the report came.

Delmar sighed and shook his head. He glanced around the bridge before grabbing the intercom.

Delmar adjusted the intercom, "Engines and weapons status, Travis."

"Engines holding for now. Working on repairing the primary weapons computer," Travis reported.

"Any chance we can get more speed?"

"The ship is already giving you 120%, Sir," Travis answered.

Delmar shook his head. They wouldn't stand a chance if he let the Coalition battle group catch up. At the same time, leaving a man behind plagued him. He glanced back once again at the remains of the enemy ship. Watching the sea claim that vessel, he gave his order.

Patrick Gloutney

WCN Hasta

Sam walked through the carrier's hangar to check up on Flint. She had just finished calming down Feather. The girl was a mess when they shut down the engines on *Feather's Edge,* but had gone from depressed to driven, forcing Sam to chase her through the aircraft carrier as she tried to find Reed. It was the most demanding she had seen Feather in a long time. She had left Feather at her bunk once Reed assured them that every effort would be made to retrieve Strafer.

With a sigh, she reached *Feather's Edge* in time to see Flint wrapping up the last steps in securing the aircraft. "Took you long enough," Flint remarked.

Sam sighed, "You know how Feather can be." There was a tense silence before Flint spoke.

"We should have waited for the restraint system to be installed."

Sam nodded again, "Wouldn't have been the worst idea."

"You know I jokingly told him not to fall out," Flint said with a grim chuckle, "Dumb ass should have listened."

"Flint—"

Flint held up her hand to stop Sam, "Don't. It was him or all of us. It...it just sucks you know?"

Sam sighed, "Yeah. I know." Sam ran her eyes over *Feather's Edge*. "Any idea what happened with the hydraulics?"

Flint rolled her neck. "Unfortunately, " the W.S.O. let out a groan. "Our EMP protections didn't work as well as we hoped. It fried some of the systems."

Sam was about to comment when someone cleared their throat, interrupting them. She turned to see Telos standing off to the side, his eyes looked hollow, and his shoulders were slumped.

"Ladies," he said, his voice lacking its usual commanding nature.

"Glad to see you made it back," Flint answered.

Telos grimaced, "How's Feather?"

"She's worried," Sam answered, "I think you are too."

Telos nodded. he was silent before he sighed, "I honestly thought Tyler putting that Phantom in the ground would be the worst we'd see."

"We don't know they're dead," Flint interjected.

Telos growled, "Rider and Gypsy are. I saw them get hit."

A stifling silence filled the air as they stood awkwardly together.

"I'm sorry, Telos," Sam said eventually.

Telos shook his head. "That's not why I'm here." Sam arched an eyebrow, "I spoke with Reed. Tyler's beacon went off."

Sam perked up, "That's great. Means he's alive! We should tell Feather."

Telos shook his head again, "The *Stanton* was attacked after we left. They suffered damage but are still sailing."

"And the *Oscoda*?" Flint asked.

"Was the ship that attacked them."

"What?" Sam asked, "But they weren't armed."

Telos shrugged, "Beats me. But with the Coalition naval group closing in...the *Stanton* can barely match their speed, assuming everything stays working as it is."

Sam swallowed, not sure she wanted to know the answer to her next question, "So what happens to Tyler?"

Telos let out a shaky sigh, "The *Stanton*'s Captain won't jeopardize his crew for the sake of one aviator. They had to leave him behind."

Sam clenched her fists. "They can't do that!"

"Yes, they can," Telos replied, "Tyler's on his own unless we do something about it."

"We?" Flint asked, resting a hand on her hip.

"How soon till *Feather's Edge* can fly?"

Flint looked to the aircraft, "I don't know. It can probably fly now. What are you thinking?"

"We need to convince Reed, but how do you feel about another rescue mission?"

Patrick Gloutney

WCN *Stanton*

"It's not just the ship anymore," Harris remarked as he and Vincent were working on repairing the primary weapons computer. They had repaired most of the system's components. Now it was just repairing the damage from the power surge to the main unit. "The crew's starting to fall apart."

Vincent removed the wire from his mouth to replace some damaged connections. "How do you mean?"

"First, the setup, the sabotage, and now LeCroix? I hope the captain can keep this ship under control," Harris explained.

Vincent shrugged, "I'm sure the captain knows what he's doing."

"Easy for you to say. You have the captain wrapped around your finger," Harris joked.

Vincent shook his head. "I simply have his guns."

Harris was silent, passing tools when asked for. "Do you think we can win this?"

Vincent paused, looking over the system he was working on. It was a haphazard mess of rewired connections, all just to have the hope of accessing their full armament. "I've seen this ship pull off some amazing feats."

"With a well-trained crew and in good working order," Harris interjected.

Vincent pulled himself out from where he was working so he could look at Harris. "You want to hear what happened when almost everyone died onboard this ship?" Harris said nothing. "You know those blue fins on the superstructure?" Harris nodded. "They weren't always there. When we first tested that weapon, they were mounted lower and more forward on the super-structure."

"Ok..." Harris trailed off, "What does that have to do with anything?"

"Those make up the primary plasma weapons array. It was top of the line at the time and still outmatches anything in service today," Vincent explained, "It's where the *Stanton* earned her nickname."

Harris cocked his head to the side, "The Ghost Ship?"

Vincent nodded, "We were on the return from an escort mission when we were ambushed. I was below decks the first time it was fired, but most of the crew were above deck. It hadn't been tested yet, but we were taking heavy fire. They had caught us by surprise, and the shield generators were damaged. The captain decided the primary plasma weapon was our best hope."

"Why was it sent out before testing?" Harris asked.

"Last-minute assignment. We were under orders not to deploy it unless necessary."

"What happened?" Harris asked.

"It worked. Too well. The placement of the array meant that the blast from the weapon obliterated every ship around us, including the ship we were escorting. Everything higher than four feet off the deck was vaporized," Vincent spoke, his voice heavy. Painful memories ran through his mind. "Some crew members were vaporized, others burned so severely they had no hope of surviving. Those in undamaged compartments were either suffocated as the fires burned up all the oxygen or burned to death. Only a handful of us survived..." Vincent trailed off; his eyes wet.

"So, the name Ghost Ship?" Harris pried.

Vincent clenched his fist, "We made it back to port even with the damage as the engines weren't hit. It took them a while to find the surviving crew. Talk of the ship being sailed back by ghosts circulated till they found out the truth."

"And they still rebuilt it after all that?" Harris asked.

Vincent nodded, "Most of our armament wasn't damaged, so I guess it was easier to repair than replace. My point is, Harris, that was a fully trained and capable crew. Delmar knows this and is careful. We just need to do our part."

Harris nodded, "You got it, boss."

Vincent slid back into the compartment he was working in. "Now if only we could get this thing working."

Harris chuckled, "At least the engines are purring nicely." There was a moment of silence before Harris banged on the compartment wall, "Shit Vincent the right engine is purring."

Vincent's eyes widened, and he tried to stand up, only to bang his head on the roof of the compartment. "What?"

"It's not groaning!" Harris called more urgently. Vincent quickly slid back out of the compartment and rushed to the engine instruments. That engine hadn't run quietly in years. He scanned the instruments looking for any sign of a problem. The temperatures were high, but that was to be expected given how hard the engines were working.

"Lower the containment wall just in case," Vincent ordered, not willing to take any chances. He watched as his crew rushed to lower the wall. As it began to slide into place, he looked to the engine. He had a terrible feeling in his gut. Vincent was about to call for the engine to be shut down when a fuel line ruptured. Fuel covered the engine quickly, saturating the air with fumes. The RPM on the starboard engine revved past the redline as the engine ingested the fumes through the failing ductwork in the engine's fresh air intake and began running away.

"Everyone get down!" Vincent ordered, just before the containment wall locked into place and the starboard engine exploded.

WCN Hasta

"What do you mean, no?" Feather asked, leaning forward on the desk towards Reed.

"Easy Feather," Sam cautioned, pulling the woman out of Reed's face.

"What about not leaving anyone behind?" she barked.

"She's got a point, Reed," Flint remarked.

"I can't risk a billion-dollar aircraft on a half-thought-out rescue attempt," Reed answered.

"You risked more than that saving the diplomats that weren't diplomats," Telos pointed out, "This mission has been a mess since the start. Don't make Strafer pay for it."

Reed balled his fists, "It's not that simple."

"Like hell it isn't," Flint remarked, "Whiteford already gave you the green light."

"No, she simply agreed to turn a blind eye. That's not approval." Reed stood to walk around the desk, "I'm just protecting everyone involved."

Sam shook her head as Telos crossed his arms, "And Strafer? He's in the water because of you."

"Pardon?" A dangerous edge in Reed's voice.

"You forced our deployment before modifications were completed on *Feather's Edge*," Telos pushed.

"He had nothing to hold on to." Flint continued.

"Well then, your pilot shouldn't have thrown him overboard," Reed shot back. Sam groaned; this was getting them nowhere.

"You son of—"

"Enough," Sam interrupted. Reed wanted to play games, so be it. "Reed is right. We stand down."

All eyes turned on Sam. She tried to ignore the hurt she saw in Feather's eyes. "What?" she asked in a quiet voice.

"Even if we could make this work, we are just as likely to have Telos fall into the water, and then what do we do?" Sam locked eyes with Telos, the man looked ready to protest, but didn't. She could see the confusion behind his eyes, but also a recognition that there was more to what Sam was playing at.

"Then I go back and pull both of them in," Flint proposed.

"That worked quite well in the practice runs, if I recall," Reed muttered.

"We can't just leave him!" Feather all but pleaded.

"We have to," Sam remarked. She saw Reed straighten up and knew she had him. "Cut our losses."

"Marshall is right. You should listen to her," Reed stated firmly, evidently feeling he had control of the situation again, "That's an order."

"But..." Flint trailed off as Sam let a smile spread on her lips.

Checkmate, Sam mused to herself. "Feather?"

"What?" Feather answered bitterly.

"Ignore Reed. Get *Feather's Edge* ready. That's an order." Sam stopped herself from smirking as she saw Reed's jaw drop. She also caught the huge grin that grew on Telos's face. Flint was the least diplomatic as she started laughing.

"You mean..." Feather asked.

"We are going to get Tyler," Sam confirmed.

Feather perked right back up and nodded, "Flint—"

"I'll pull the covers and start the checks. You get the walk around," Flint finished for her, holding the door open. In the blink of an eye, they were both rushing down the hall.

"What the hell just happened?" Reed asked.

"Exactly what you ordered." Sam scowled before stepping out into the hallway. Telos followed shortly afterward.

"That took balls, Greaser," he remarked as they made their way towards the flight deck. "He's going to come after you for that one."

Sam nodded, "Let's just hope that Whiteford keeps her word about no court-martials."

Patrick Gloutney

WCN *Stanton*

The sudden deceleration that followed the sound of an explosion knocked Delmar off his feet. He groaned, picking himself off the floor.

"Report?" he ordered.

"Starboard engine has stopped responding, sir."

"Active Fire Alarms in the engine room."

"Any radar or sonar contacts?" Delmar asked. He couldn't understand how they had missed an oncoming attack.

"Just the Coalition battle group, and they are still outside their weapons range."

"Then what hit us?" Delmar asked. There was no response from any sailor on the bridge. "Then find out." Delmar hit the intercom, "Travis, report."

There was no response from the engine room. "Travis, status report," Delmar tried again. Again, no answer.

"Sir," a sailor called, "The fire's spreading. Alarms are now active in compartments forward of the engine room."

Delmar shook his head, "Travis I need a damn report!" No response, "What's our current speed?"

"We are down to 18 knots, Sir. The coalition battle group is closing on our position. Estimate a couple of hours before they are within firing range."

"Time till our ships reach us?"

"At least three hours."

Delmar shook his head. *This is going to end up being a standoff with us caught in the crossfire.* They needed air cover, but that would be useless against another EMP attack unless he could get those fighters from the rescue mission back. Delmar drummed his fingers on the console in front of him.

"Get me the command of the Hasta Battlegroup," he ordered. He needed to buy time, and he needed to do it now. If they were to have any hope of getting the *Stanton* back to port, they needed to somehow delay the Coalition battlegroup. "And would someone please get me a status report on the engine room?"

"Sir! You're needed on the rear deck," a call came.

Delmar looked up, "The rear deck?"

"Yes, Sir, there's something you need to see," the sailor answered. Delmar nodded and followed the sailor off the bridge.

"One of the boys noticed it after the explosion. Came right up through the deck," the sailor explained, walking at a brisk pace.

"Up through the deck?" Delmar matched the man's pace. "Is it a shell?"

The sailor shook his head, "Not like one I've ever seen, Sir."

Delmar's jaw fell open when they reached the rear decks. A large deformed piece of metal sat wedged in the ship's deck; the surrounding metal pushed outwards as if the object had pierced the hull from the keel up. It sent a worrisome thought through Delmar's mind. If it had done that, then they were certainly taking on water.

"What do you think it is, Sir?" the sailor asked. Delmar studied the object for a few moments before shaking his head.

"You're right, it's not a shell," he stated. They hadn't been hit by anything. A terrible feeling settled in Delmar's gut. "It's the cylinder head off one of our engines." They had blown up their engine room.

Feather's Edge

"Clear one," Feather called.

"Starting one," Sam answered as she engaged the starter on the left-hand engine of *Feather's Edge*. They had gotten *Feather's Edge* ready to fly rather quickly, all things considered. Sam was still cautious as she ran through the system checks on startup. Flint had assured her that they had fixed most of the issues they had encountered on their last flight. The fact that she had used the word "most" however, did not escape her.

"After start checks complete," Sam reported to Feather who nodded. Sam glanced around the hangar deck; she was worried Reed would try and stop them before they got the chance to depart. No doubt he was on the sat phone with Command right now.

"Pre-takeoff checks," Feather called.

"Complete," Sam answered a moment later. "All systems green for departure."

"Hang on, Tyler. We're coming," Sam heard Feather whisper. She glanced back at Flint, who just shrugged. Sam chewed on her cheek. It wasn't that she thought this was a bad idea, but she worried Feather might be letting her feelings impede her judgment.

"Feather," She started, "You know he may not take you back after we rescue him."

Feather nodded and sighed heavily, "I know, but that doesn't mean I'm going to leave him to drown."

"I'm with Feather," Flint called from behind them, "At least he's alive if he hates our guts."

Sam shook her head but smiled, "Just don't get your hopes up."

"I won't," Feather stated, placing her hand on the throttles.

Movement caught Sam's eye as she looked back outside, "Shit." Armed soldiers had surrounded *Feather's Edge*, their guns trained on the cockpit.

"*Feather's Edge,* you are ordered to shut down your engines and exit your aircraft," a voice called over the radio.

"Looks like Reed wore the captain down," Flint remarked.

"Damage estimates from those weapons?" Feather asked.

Sam raised an eyebrow, "You planning on disobeying and running?"

"Significant if they hit our engines," Flint answered before Feather could.

"*Feather's Edge,* shut down your engines or you will be fired upon," the controller's voice called again. Sam caught sight of one of the anti-aircraft guns swinging around to face them. *Reed would rather destroy us than take a chance on saving Strafer.*

Sam noted how tightly Feather was gripping the throttle. She could only imagine the turmoil going on in her friend's head. She scanned the group of armed guards again. She locked eyes with one of them. The man motioned his weapon towards the sea and mouthed the words "Go."

"Marshaller giving us the go for take-off," Feather remarked. A marshaller was signalling their take-off clearance.

"*Feather's Edge,* this is your final warning."

The ACARS system beeped, signalling a new message had been received. Sam quickly glanced at the display, and her eyes widened. The message read:

I've got your back — Whiteford

Sam heard a couple of breakers pop behind her, followed by a warning horn.

"Com systems offline," Flint reported. Sam glanced at Feather.

"That's unfortunate. Greaser, confirm take-off clearance," Feather quickly shot back.

Sam glanced back at the marshaller, "Confirmed."

"Power's set. Liftoff," Feather called, advancing the throttles and lifting the aircraft off the deck. "Ready countermeasures."

"Armed." Sam braced herself for the attack that was sure to follow from essentially stealing a top-secret aircraft. The weapons fire never came.

Patrick Gloutney

WCN *Stanton*

"Travis, status report," Delmar's voice commanded as Vincent shook his head, trying to clear his vision. His ears were ringing from the explosion. The lights in the control room flickered, barely lighting the area as he pulled himself to his feet. What he saw looking out at the engine room floor was complete and utter devastation. The containment wall for the starboard engine had blown off its rails. It looked like it had been shredded by the explosion. Fires raged, casting an eerie glow in the poorly lit compartment. The fire suppression system struggled to put out the tangled mass of metal that had once been their starboard engine. And the bodies, a scene not unlike his nightmares, were laid out in front of Vincent. Men and women lay burned and broken in heaps on the floor.

"Travis, I need a damn report!" Delmar's voice came again. Travis couldn't bring himself to even speak. A sob came from his throat as he was forced once again to relive that day. Once again, losing a crew. The *Stanton* brought nothing but death to those who sailed her blindly, and torment for those who survived. He collapsed on the floor.

"Travis!" Harris's voice called faintly over the ringing in his ears. A set of hands grabbed Vincent. "Travis, are you alright?" Travis could only shake his head, tears flowing down his cheeks.

"It's ok," Harris reassured.

Travis shook his head again, "Should have—"

"Stop," Harris scolded. "What happened?"

Travis shrugged, "Engine blew...they're all dead."

Harris shook Vincent, "Snap out of it, Vincent. The rest of the crew isn't." Vincent was going to protest when Harris shook him again. "But we will be if you don't pull it together."

Vincent steeled his nerves and nodded. He forced himself to compartmentalize; just like every morning. *Focus on those you can save;* he turned back to the engine room floor. The damage was extensive but a glance at the port engine's instruments revealed it was still operating within limitations. The fire suppression system had done its job and the fires were gone for now. "Inspection...we need to do an inspection."

"Agreed," Harris called, handing Vincent a flashlight. They rushed to the damaged engine. Vincent looked over it quickly, but it was a total loss. He was about to go inspect the still-running unit when Harris called out.

"Holy hell." Vincent followed Harris's light, and his jaw dropped. There was a massive hole in the ceiling. "That explains where the rest of the engine is."

Vincent nodded, "We need to protect that port engine. If it's damaged, we can't have it blowing up like this one."

"Maybe we should shut it down," Harris suggested.

Vincent chewed on his lip, normally that would be the proper course of action but given the circumstances... "Delmar needs all the speed we can give him. We shut it down we are all dead."

Harris seemed about to protest before he nodded. Vincent took a step towards the running engine only to feel water splash against his leg. "Shit." Vincent pointed his light to the ground, and sure enough, water was swirling at their feet.

"Oh, this is bad," Harris stated. Vincent nodded, shining his light on the aft part of the compartment. He cursed as it illuminated the leak. Water sprayed in through the drive shaft seal for the starboard prop.

"The blast must have torqued the shaft and blown the seals," Vincent remarked.

"We can fix that, right?"

"You got a dry dock anywhere?" Vincent asked.

Harris shook his head.

Vincent made his way back to the control room for the intercom, "Engine room to Bridge."

The response from the Bridge seemed to take forever, "Travis, you have no idea how good it is to hear you. Status on your crew?"

Vincent looked back out over the bodies, chewing on his cheek. Harris stepped up and queued the intercom, "Heavy casualties, Sir."

Silence reigned in the engine room as Vincent shook his head, repressing his memories and focusing on the task at hand.

"Damage report?" Delmar asked finally.

Vincent grabbed the mic, "Starboard engine is a complete loss. The port engine is still running."

"Can we get any more speed out of it?" Delmar asked.

"Negative. It's already at max continuous power. Pushing it beyond that is too dangerous."

"Travis," Harris called, "The flooding."

Vincent nodded, "It gets worse, Captain."

"Worse than blowing up an engine?"

"We are taking on water, Sir."

"Patch the leak," Delmar instructed.

"Negative, Sir. It's too severe."

Harris leaned against the console. "Any more tricks up your sleeve, Travis?"

Vincent shook his head, "I wish I knew."

"What do you need, Travis?" Delmar's voice asked. "Manpower? Tools? Tell me what you need to keep this ship afloat."

Travis looked over the damaged engine room. Keeping the *Stanton* afloat was a tall order now. If they could just keep it above water long enough to reach the carrier fleet headed their way, they would have a chance, "Any sailor who has a mechanical background. I need more than two hands for the inspections."

"You'll have them." Delmar answered, "And medics for you and Harris."

Vincent turned to Harris, "How do you feel about MacGyver?"

Harris raised an eyebrow. "Why?"

"Find anything that can be turned into a bilge pump." Vincent instructed, "We may not be able to stop the flooding, but we can at least slow it down."

Eastern Coalition Assault Vessel

Tyler shivered as he wrestled with the ropes binding his hands together as he sat on the bow of the small watercraft. From what he could tell, it was some sort of armed landing craft. It was filled with the crew from the Eastern Coalition ship that had posed as the *Oscoda*. He hissed as the rope cut into his wrists.

"That won't do any good," one of the crew said as he sat next to Tyler.

Tyler stopped his struggle and sighed, "Good to see someone speaks English."

The man nodded, "Not many. Water?"

Tyler eagerly took the offered bottle without thinking. The water helped to soothe his dry throat. "Thanks."

The man smiled, taking the canteen back, "Just ask if you want more."

Tyler cocked his head to the side, "What about the others?"

The man shrugged, "They each have water." Tyler raised an eyebrow. Was this man giving him some of his allowances? "Do not look so shocked. We are not monsters." Tyler wasn't sure how to answer that. "Here." The man leaned forward and untied the ropes around Tyler's wrists.

"What are you doing?" Tyler asked. Surely this man realized that untying a captive could lead to any number of problems.

The man simply laughed, "You planning on running?" He then gestured to the open ocean, "Be my guest." Tyler glanced around at the other men. To his surprise, none seemed to be giving him any attention. "We did not pull you from the water to hurt you."

"Then why?" Tyler asked.

The man raised an eyebrow, "I like to think you'd do the same for a drowning man abandoned by his people."

Tyler let out a sigh and leaned back. He was silent for a while. His thoughts turned to watching both *Feather's Edge* and the *Stanton* disappear off into the distance. *Why didn't they turn back for me?* He could understand *Feather's Edge*; they were likely low on fuel, but surely the *Stanton* could have done something. He looked back at the man he had been talking with.

"Thank you then," he said eventually.

The man nodded, "Call me Yuri."

"Tyler." The two men lapsed back into silence. Tyler rolled his neck, he had so many questions about this whole mission. He wondered if he'd even make it home. He doubted all of the Coalition crews were as accommodating as Yuri.

"What happened to the real *Oscoda?*" Tyler asked eventually.

Yuri was quiet for a moment. "Despite what you might think, we are not looking for war, Tyler."

"You sank it, didn't you?"

"Before it joined up with the *Stanton*," Yuri sighed, "Would you think twice about sinking my ship when ordered to?" Tyler looked away. He couldn't refute that. "You would know my ship as the *Chimera*. It is a spy ship primarily."

"Well armed for a spy vessel," Tyler remarked. He had heard about the *Chimera*. The war had captivated the imaginations of the public, turning ships and aircraft into legends over the years. The *Chimera* was rumoured to be the most prolific spy vessel the Eastern Coalition had, having infiltrated and gathered more information than any other intelligence asset.

Yuri shook his head, "We were retrofitted with heavy armament just for this mission. None of the crew were eager to sink the *Oscoda,* but orders are orders."

"Why all the cloak and daggers?" Tyler asked.

Yuri cocked his head to one side, "I do not understand."

"Why the tricks? Why send such a large military force after something that wasn't even a threat?"

"Wasn't a threat?" Yuri asked. "You mean my ship?"

Tyler nodded, "Seems silly to attack your men."

Yuri nodded, "It would be. The *Chimera* was not the target, though. We wanted the *Stanton.* We just needed you all to think it was us."

"The *Stanton?*"

Yuri sat up a bit straighter, "We tricked your people into sending out an escort group with false promises of a peace treaty. The diplomats on the *Oscoda* made sure the *Stanton* was part of that group. We had intended to trick your people into thinking it had been sunk so we could capture it."

"Why? I thought it was useless."

"Useless? It cut my ship in half," Yuri shook his head. "Do you know what the *Stanton* really is? We call it a harbinger of death."

"It's an old warship. Isn't it?"

"An old warship with weapons of mass destruction on board," Yuri explained. "Have you ever wondered why this war has dragged out for so long? Our governments refuse to back down, as do yours, but we fear provoking your government. Imagine one ship against an armada of our navy, and in the blink of an eye, every one of my ships is turned to dust."

"Sounds like science fiction," Tyler remarked.

Yuri shook his head, a grim expression etched across his face, "We lost many ships and aircraft to the *Stanton* over the years. It is no fiction."

"So why the attack now?"

"Intelligence reports led us to believe the *Stanton* was to be retired. We jumped at the opportunity to get the technology for ourselves – a way to level the playing field. Our intelligence was sadly wrong when it came to the ship's capabilities."

Tyler mulled over this new information, "Why tell me all this?"

Yuri shrugged, "You were caught in the crossfire. You deserved to know why. As I said, we are not monsters."

"How do you know all this?" Tyler pushed, "Seems like a lot of classified information."

Yuri grinned, "I'm the Captain of the *Chimera*."

Tyler's eyes widened. The Captain of the *Chimera* was rumoured to be a ruthless man to outsiders. Taking the life of anyone who discovered the true identity of his ship. He was also known as a man whose every action had meaning.

Yuri nodded, "I see you've heard of my reputation. It's easy to see how rumours grow and change until they represent nothing of reality, is it not?"

Tyler nodded, trying to figure out why this man had pulled him from the water, "You're using me as bait, aren't you?"

Yuri shrugged again, "As I said, I wished only to help. If the *Stanton* returns for you and puts itself within our grasp, that would be...what do you call it, a happy accident?"

Shouting from the other crew on the landing boat drew Tyler's attention toward the stern. Every man was getting to their feet, raising their weapons. Off in the distance, he could make out an aircraft coming towards them.

"I see your people have come for you after all," Yuri remarked, getting to his feet. Tyler watched as the aircraft's shape grew. He felt a mix of unease and relief as he realized it was *Feather's Edge*. The aircraft soon sped overhead; the landing craft pulling a wide arcing turn to the left. It swung around and pulled into a hover, slowly approaching them.

Yuri backed orders over the noise of the engines. Tyler glanced at the other men; they all stood with weapons at the ready, worry and nerves etched on their faces, but none fired. Yuri was smart; he knew *Feather's Edge* wouldn't fire unless fired upon. Tyler's gaze moved to the cockpit of the aircraft. He locked eyes with Claire, she put a hand on the glass in front of her. She had come back for him, despite everything; she had come back.

The moment was shattered as Tyler saw dread seep into Claire's expression a second before a muzzle of a gun pressed against the back of his neck. He looked back at Yuri.

"I am sorry," the man said simply, "Orders."

Tyler looked back at Claire. If this were to be the end, he wanted her to be the last thing he saw. A shot erupted from the cannons on *Feather's Edge,* and the muzzle disappeared from Tyler's neck. Gunfire erupted from the landing craft. *Feather's Edge* swung around, its guns peppering the landing craft, leaving large holes in the panels. The crew ducked out of the way. Tyler looked back to see Claire motioning to the water.

"Jump," she mouthed the words through the glass. Tyler swallowed, jumping back into the water was the last thing he wanted to do. A glance at the landing craft and the crew getting back to their feet made it an easy choice, however.

The water was cold, just as cold as before. Tyler swam as fast as he could away from the landing craft. He could hear more gunfire exchanged between *Feather's Edge* and the *Chimera* crew. Finally, after he felt he couldn't swim any further, he stopped. Tyler let himself float in the water, the waves rocking him, water lapping up over his mouth and nose. He could see *Feather's Edge* moving nearer to him. Its ramp opened to reveal Telos tossing a rope ladder down. Tyler willed his body to move, despite the cold and downwash from the rotors, making it hard to get to the ladder. Partway up, Telos hauled him the rest of the way.

"We've got him! Go, go, go!" Tyler heard Telos call as he raised the ramp. Tyler could feel the aircraft bank steeply and accelerate. He just let himself lie on the floor of the cargo hold, shivering. Telos placed a blanket on him. "Damn you're a sight for sore eyes."

Tyler nodded, pulling the blanket tight, "The...the others?" Telos didn't answer. Instead, he helped Tyler into a seat, "Telos?"

"Rest," Telos ordered, "We can worry about everything else later."

WCN *Stanton*

Vincent unceremoniously fell onto a seat in the engine control room. Harris wasn't far behind him.

Harris let out a brief chuckle as he dumped the water out of his boot, "The stories I'll tell my grandchildren."

Vincent glanced, stifling a yawn, "About how your ship tried to kill you?"

Harris shook his head, sending water all over, "About how I saved a sinking ship with a blender."

Despite the situation, Vince let loose a tired laugh, "That's a slight exaggeration."

Harris seemed to think on that for a moment, "I mean, we used the motor from a blender."

Vincent shook his head but smiled, "I guess. At least we've slowed the flooding somewhat."

"What's next?" Harris asked as he undid his other boot.

Vincent scanned over the instrument panel next to him. There was so much left to do. They had bought themselves time, but the *Stanton* was still very much sinking.

"I think a break for both of you," Delmar said, stepping into the room. Harris gave a weary salute to the captain, but the fact that he didn't stand spoke volumes. It stopped Vincent's protests in his throat.

"He's right, Harris. Get some rest. The extra hands the captain lent us can take it from here," Vincent instructed.

"What about you?" Harris asked.

Vincent looked away. He hated being hypocritical. "Go while we still have a handle on things. I'll send for you if I need you."

Harris seemed about to protest, but a look from the captain made him nod and take his leave. Delmar took a seat where Harris had been.

"I want you and Harris on rotating shifts. You're no good to us, exhausted."

"So, you've said," Vincent responded, "How bad is our situation?"

Delmar shook his head. "I want to know how bad your situation is first."

Vincent arched an eyebrow, "The seal is—"

"No, Travis," Delmar interrupted, "You personally. I can't imagine finding your crew dead was easy on you, especially considering your past."

Vincent looked away from Delmar. He fought to keep the memories away, "Nothing I haven't seen before, Sir."

"Doesn't make it any easier, Travis," Delmar pushed.

"Then don't make me relive it!" Travis snapped. He then shrank back at the surprised expression on Delmar's face. "Sorry, Sir."

Delmar nodded, "Very well. Take care of yourself."

Vincent nodded and quickly changed the subject, "I'm not sure I can fix that leak."

Delmar seemed to take the hint: "How would we fare in a fight against a Coalition battle group?"

Vincent reached for a waterlogged report he had drawn up, "We would need a Hail Mary. We are running on a damaged main generator and the backup systems."

Delmar nodded, taking the report, "I imagine that's taken a toll on our armament."

Vincent nodded, "Significantly. You can only use one shield at a time, and maybe 50% of the plasma weapons. EMP are out of the question now, too."

"Two ships on either side of us would be the end of it all," Delmar remarked, "Almost all of our conventional weapons are damaged as well."

"We put up one hell of a fight, Sir," Vincent started rubbing his forehead.

"That we did," Delmar muttered before he sighed, "Travis, unless we can reach our ships in the next couple of hours...I may have to consider surrendering the *Stanton* to the Eastern Coalition."

Vincent shot straight up in his seat, "Sir, you can't—"

"I can if it means that the rest of the crew survives."

Vincent shook his head, "But the technology onboard. It could turn the tables on the war."

Delmar nodded, "I'm open to suggestions."

Vincent chewed on his lip and glanced at the engine instruments. They were already pushing their last engine as fast as they could go. His eyes fell on a control panel for the rapid repositioning thrusters.

"I might have a way to make that work, but it's risky."

Delmar raised an eyebrow, "I'm all ears."

"We could re-angle the repositioning thrusters. Use them as our main propulsion," Vincent explained. "It would get you more than enough speed."

Delmar nodded, "And the risks?"

Vincent chuckled darkly, "It's never been tested. I don't know what the condition of our frame is. The forces might tear the ship apart or breach our hull."

"Sounds like an act of desperation," Delmar sighed, "But I'm a desperate man. Make it so, Travis."

Patrick Gloutney

Feather's Edge

The rotors slowed to a stop as Sam wrapped up the last of her shutdown checks. She let out a sigh of relief as she placed the checklist in its place, "Shut down checks complete."

"You have control," Feather stated as she nearly threw her restraints off and pulled herself out of her seat.

Sam grabbed her arm, "Feather, you don't know what you might find back there."

"I don't care!" Feather snapped. "I need to see him."

Sam nodded and released Feather. She disappeared seconds later. Sam chewed on her lip, shaking her head as she started securing the cockpit.

"I hope Strafer knows how lucky he is," Flint remarked.

Sam nodded. She did one last check of everything and undid her restraints. As she climbed out of her seat, she saw Flint eying her, helmet resting on the W.S.O. console. "What?"

"That was incredibly risky what you did."

Sam looked away, "Maybe. Doesn't matter, it worked."

Flint shook her head, "They didn't fire first, Sam."

Sam locked eyes with Flint, "I wasn't about to let Feather watch her boyfriend's brains get splattered on our windshield."

Flint nodded, "I'm not saying it was wrong, but it's a violation of our rules of engagement."

Sam cocked an eyebrow, "And stealing this bird is perfectly fine though, right?"

Flint chuckled, "I'm just saying I expect more leniency next time I don't play by the rules, Miss 'by the book'."

Sam shook her head, "After this week. Sure, why not?"

Flint undid her restraints. "If they ask, though, we didn't take the first shot."

"Of course, we didn't," Sam answered matter-of-factly, "That would be against our rules of engagement."

"Good, now let's get out of here," Flint said, motioning for Sam to move. As they emerged from *Feather's Edge,* they were greeted by the sight of a ship on high alert. A palpable tension was in the air as every weapon Sam could see was trained off in the distance from which they had come. She glanced around and noticed that every other ship in the battle group was doing the same. The missile frigates even had their silo bay doors open.

"What did we miss?" Flint asked as they saw Telos.

"Something fast is coming our way. They thought the radar return was the *Stanton,* but after the *Oscoda,* no one knows what to believe anymore," Telos explained.

"How's Strafer?" Sam asked.

"Shaken, but he'll live. Good flying by the way."

"At least we didn't drop you," Sam remarked.

"Why don't they just shoot it?" Flint asked as she eyed up one of the frigates, "Seems stupid to let it get close."

Telos shrugged, "Maybe they don't want to accidentally sink the *Stanton.*"

"Still seems risky," Flint remarked.

"Telos?" Sam asked, "Is Feather with Strafer?" Telos nodded. "Is he still mad at her?"

Telos shrugged, "Hurt, but not mad. I don't think they will be back to normal after this if that's what you are asking."

Sam nodded; it was better than him outright hating her.

"Holy shit," Flint remarked, pointing to the horizon, "How is that possible?"

Sam looked and noticed a dot on the horizon. She looked closer and her eyes widened. In the distance, a large warship was crashing through the swells at an incredible speed. Sam noticed the weapons on their carrier re-aimed towards the ship. "I've never seen a ship move that fast."

"I hope it's ours," Telos remarked.

The dot grew, and before long, they could see it crashing hard into each wave, almost skimming the tops of each swell. It was behaving more like a small speedboat than a warship.

"It's heading right for us," Telos observed seconds before the collision alarm sounded and the carrier's deck pitched suddenly in a rapid turn. As Sam regained her footing, she looked to see the whole battlegroup breaking away into turns to avoid the rapidly approaching vessel. The large warship careened past them, just missing the carrier and another destroyer, before a loud bang sounded through the air. Everyone on deck rushed to the other side of the carrier.

There, slowing, in the middle of the battle group, its turrets bent and mangled into nearly unrecognizable masses of metal, burn marks covering its decks and hull, while black smoke seeped out of what looked like rockets on the rear of the superstructure, sat the *Stanton*.

Patrick Gloutney

WCN *Stanton*

Delmar glanced at the men gathered in his quarters. He could tell Travis was about ready to chew General Reed's head off. "Absolutely not," Delmar said finally.

"It would work." Reed insisted.

"Travis?" Delmar asked.

Travis shook his head, "Our hull is too heavily compromised from our high-speed run here."

Delmar put the pen he was holding on his desk. He watched as it rolled off the table, "Hence our list. A high-speed tow is out of the question."

"What about your engines?" Captain Mangan of the Hasta asked.

"We can't get enough speed out of our remaining engine to stay ahead of the Coalition battle group," Delmar explained.

"What about the rapid position thrusters?" Reed asked.

Delmar looked to Travis; the man seemed to watch him for permission to speak. Delmar nodded. Travis took a breath, "We burnt them out with the ride here. They won't relight."

"We better come up with something soon," Mangan observed, "The Coalition ships are within firing range."

"Standoff it is then," Reed remarked. "The *Stanton* can hold them off."

Delmar caught Travis shaking his head, "I doubt it, sir," Delmar spoke, "We've lost most of our armament."

Reed cocked an eyebrow and turned to Travis, "You let everything fail." Delmar didn't miss the choice of wording on Reed's part.

Travis sighed, "We don't have the power for the weapons – not without the second engine."

Reed shook his head, "Unbelievable. You had one job. What are our options?"

"If we lock horns with the Coalition battle group, it's going to mean heavy casualties on both sides," Mangan stated. "What if we just let the *Stanton* sink?"

Reed shook his head, "Not an option. They don't want it sunk; they want it captured. We'd be handing it right over to them."

"There is a way to scuttle it," Travis spoke up. Delmar didn't miss the glare Reed shot him.

"What do you propose?" Delmar asked before Reed could speak.

"Fire the primary plasma array with the shields up. It would turn the ship to dust."

Delmar leaned forward in his chair. "I thought the shields were offline?"

Travis nodded, "For continued use. I can rig enough power from the remaining generator to make this work."

"Why not do this before?" Mangan asked.

"It won't last," Travis explained, "It will blow the generator out, once I fire it. The residual power will hold the shields long enough for the blast to destroy the Stanton."

Delmar shook his head; he didn't like where this was going. Reed, on the other hand, looked elated. "I like it."

Man thinks of no one but himself, Delmar thought, "Gentlemen, may I have a moment with my Chief Engineer?"

Mangan and Reed nodded, "Just make it work." With that, they left. When the door closed, Delmar turned to Travis.

"I don't like it."

"You don't have to. But you can see it's the only way," Travis responded.

"Correct me if I am wrong, but someone would have to be on board to fire the weapons, right?"

Travis nodded, leaning against the wall, "Correct."

"Hell of a suicide," Delmar remarked.

"Sacrifice," Travis corrected.

"No, it's damn suicide, Vincent," Delmar snapped, "We find another way."

Travis leaned over the table towards Delmar, "There's no other way Captain." A tense silence filled the air till Travis sighed, "Apply the same logic you did with that airman we left behind. One life to save every sailor onboard."

Delmar groaned, "Travis—"

"I am not worth any more than anyone else on this ship," Travis interrupted, "I am also the only one who can do this. That can keep us safe from the *Stanton's* weapons once and for all."

Delmar locked eyes with Travis. He could see the determination behind his engineer's eyes, but also a barely contained fear. Travis looked terrified of what might happen if his plan didn't go through.

"It's the whole reason I stayed on board this long. Let me do this," Travis pushed. He then pulled the picture of his dead girlfriend and slapped it on the desk, "For the crew, for her. Let me make sure this damn ship is finished once and for all."

Delmar sighed, "You deserve a damn medal."

"Not with my record," Travis answered back quickly. "Abandon the ship and end this madness."

Delmar looked to Travis, "Captains go down with their ships."

"Call it extenuating circumstances," Travis shot back quickly, "I will not fire those weapons with anyone else onboard. Crew leaves, you included."

Delmar sighed and ran a hand through his hair. The airman had been easy, simple math. Plus, he didn't know the man. Travis was different. After everything he had done, he didn't deserve to die with the *Stanton*. Delmar also knew they wouldn't stand a chance if the Eastern Coalition duplicated the technology onboard. "You shouldn't order your Captain."

Travis tensed, "This is something I have to stand firm on, Sir."

Delmar shook his head. He looked back at the determination and fear in Travis's eyes. With a heavy heart, he gave his order.

WCN Hasta

Tyler looked across the water at the beaten warship rocking in the swells. The longer he looked at it, the worse the damage seemed. From burn marks to twisted masses of metal that used to be weapons, not to mention the noticeable list to one side that the ship had. Tyler hung his head. He was still bitter about it, but he could understand why the captain had left him behind. Questions still burned in his mind, however.

"Hey," Claire's soft voice called from beside him as she placed a hand on the railing, "How are you feeling?"

Tyler shrugged, "Clean bill of health."

Claire nodded, "You're allowed to be shaken."

Tyler sighed, eyes still fixed on the *Stanton,* "It just doesn't make sense."

"What doesn't?"

"The *Oscoda,* or *Chimera.* If the diplomats were prisoners of war, why allow them to be taken by *Feather's Edge?* Why not keep them on the *Chimera* and shoot us down?"

Claire shrugged, "Orders don't always make sense – especially taken out of context."

Tyler turned on Claire, "Yet you follow them. To the letter."

Claire flinched, "I'm sorry, Tyler."

Tyler shook his head, "It was never going to work anyway. We would have been reassigned at some point."

Claire looked towards the *Stanton*, "I disobeyed orders to come to get you."

Tyler raised an eyebrow. "Sorry?"

"We were ordered to stand down. We were even held at gunpoint. We came for you regardless," Claire explained.

Tyler leaned against the ship's railing. He eyed Claire, trying to see if she was telling the truth, "I thought that wasn't possible."

Claire nodded, "It's not supposed to be. But I couldn't let you drown." Claire then turned back to face Tyler, "I know I am not what you were hoping for. I wasn't honest with you, and I ended things over a stupid directive. But Tyler, you are everything to me. I'd sever my connection with *Feather's Edge* if it meant I could have you back."

Tyler shook his head, "Claire..."

"I'm not asking for us to go back to normal, but to try again. Now that you know what to expect. Give me a chance to earn you back."

"Until you're ordered otherwise," Tyler sighed, "That's a very unhealthy approach to a relationship, Claire."

Claire was silent for a moment, before she took Tyler's hand in hers, "You are one thing I can disobey orders for."

Tyler looked at her hand and sighed. He knew it was only opening himself up to more betrayal and pain. It would be foolish to go back into a relationship with someone so fickle. But at the same time, something in her eyes made him trust her, just as he had before.

"Fine," Tyler said finally, "But no debts. We start fresh. Equal ground. No one is winning anyone back. Agreed?"

Claire nodded, "I can live with that."

WCN Hasta

"Looks like it was one hell of a ride," Captain Mangan remarked as she joined Delmar on the *Hasta's* catwalk.

"You could say that," Delmar answered, looking over the *Stanton* from afar.

"LeCroix wants your head, you know," Mangan continued.

"I don't blame him," Delmar answered quickly as his eyes drifted to the deck of the carrier. He caught Harris looking up at him. The engineer locked eyes with Delmar before looking away. He had not been in support of Travis's plan.

"He's calling for me to throw you in the brig," Mangan continued.

Delmar turned toward the fellow Captain, "Are you going to?"

Mangan shook her head, "I'm sure you had your reasons for removing him from command. Personally, if you don't trust him, I don't trust him."

Delmar chuckled, "You barely know me."

Mangan shrugged and motioned to the damaged *Stanton*, "Any Captain that brings a ship that beaten up back and gets most of his crew off safely deserves some faith, I think."

Delmar shook his head, his eyes drifting back to the *Stanton*, "Not everyone. Ever have to leave anyone behind, Mangan?"

Mangan shook her head this time, "Thankfully, no."

Delmar sighed and straightened up, "I'm not the reason that ship is here right now. Travis is. And now I'm letting him die."

"You are doing what's best for your crew and country," Mangan protested, "It's unfortunate that this is what it is. He's a brave man."

Delmar shook his head, "I wish that were the case. He's brave, don't get me wrong. But he's doing this out of fear."

"Why would you say that?" Mangan asked.

"I am not foolish enough to think that LeCroix is only calling for my head," Delmar remarked, "Travis knows he's going to be court-martialed. He has so little faith in our military that he fears the retribution he might face." Mangan remained silent as Delmar gripped the railing. "How have we screwed up so bad that it's easier for Travis to die with that ship than come home?"

"And you?" Mangan asked finally.

"Pardon?"

"You'll be court-martialed. Not just for LeCroix but for the loss of the *Stanton*. Do you share his fear?" Mangan asked.

Delmar shook his head, "It's different for me. I have reason to trust the system. We all lost Travis's trust a long time ago." The two Captains fell silent, just the sound of the wind and the bustle of the carrier. "The man deserves a damn medal, but with his service record he'll be lucky if his name is even mentioned to Whiteford."

"Excuse me," Mangan stated, stepping back onto the bridge. Delmar barely acknowledged her as he looked out at the *Stanton*. The shield generators were extending from the ship's hull. Delmar could almost hear the alarms warning of the impending weapons discharge. It was then that Delmar made a promise to himself.

It's not in vain, Delmar told himself; Travis was ensuring the technology on the *Stanton* wouldn't be replicated. And Delmar would assure the treatment of Vincent Travis in the military was brought to light.

The two frigates flanking the *Stanton* let loose a shot each into the air. The echo of cannon fire reverberated across the ships in the battle group. It shook Delmar from his reprieve. The second set of shots was fired as Mangan walked back to his side.

"It's not a twenty-one-gun salute," Mangan said as the third set of shots fired and the blue fins on the *Stanton* started to glow. "But it will have to do." The fourth volley of shots erupted as the other ships in the battle group joined in. Delmar nodded his approval and came to attention. He and Mangan snapped to a crisp salute as the light from the *Stanton's* fins grew. Then, as the fifth volley of shots erupted, so did a flash of pale blue light. When it cleared the *Stanton* and Travis, along with it, were gone.

Acknowledgments

I would like to acknowledge the contributions of Sharyn Heagle, who provided moral and technical support, along with knowledge to which I would not otherwise have had access. Without her, this book would not have been possible. Thank you to my mother, Betty Gloutney, to Melody Tomka and my loving wife, Aldirene Gloutney, for their assistance in editing this manuscript. Finally, thanks to my family and friends who stood behind me and put up with the process of my writing this manuscript. Thanks to you all.

Born in Nova Scotia, Patrick Gloutney always held an interest in storytelling:
Putting pen to paper at a relatively young age. After moving to Ottawa, and
interest in writing grew. He was awarded 2nd place in the National Capital Youth
Writing Competition in 2013. He continues to explore various approaches to
writing alongside pursuing his other passion, aviation. An active member of the
flying community, he has been repeatedly recognized for his dedication, en-
thusiasm, and professionalism in his craft.

www.ingramcontent.com/pod-product-compliance
Lightning Source LLC
Chambersburg PA
CBHW020616180626
46810CB00007B/2807